ZAPPED

**Center Point
Large Print**

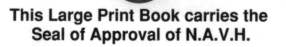

**This Large Print Book carries the
Seal of Approval of N.A.V.H.**

ZAPPED

A Regan Reilly Mystery

Carol Higgins Clark

CENTER POINT PUBLISHING
THORNDIKE, MAINE

This Center Point Large Print edition
is published in the year 2008 by arrangement with
Scribner, a division of Simon & Schuster, Inc.

Copyright © 2008 by Carol Higgins Clark.

All rights reserved.

ISBN: 978-1-60285-202-0

Library of Congress Cataloging-in-Publication Data

Clark, Carol Higgins.
    Zapped / Carol Higgins Clark.--Center Point large print ed.
      p. cm.
    ISBN 978-1-60285-202-0 (lib. bdg. : alk. paper)
    1. Reilly, Regan (Fictitious character)--Fiction. 2. Women private investigators--New York
(State)--New York--Fiction. 3. New York (N.Y.)--Fiction. 4. Large type books. I. Title.

PS3553.L278Z37 2008
813'.54--dc22

2008010923

Acknowledgments

Starting a book is not unlike being thrown into a blackout. The following people helped me find my way through the dark!

First, I'd like to express my gratitude to my editor, Roz Lippel. As usual, Roz, it's been wonderful working with you.

My agent, Esther Newberg.

My publicist, Lisl Cade.

Associate Director of Copyediting Gypsy da Silva, copyeditor Tony Newfield, and proofreaders Barbara Raynor and Steve Friedeman.

Art Director John Fulbrook III, photographer Glenn Jussen, and Glenn's wife, Belle.

Scribner Publishing Manager Kara Watson.

A special thanks to Mike Clendenin and Katherine Boden from Con Edison who were so gracious in taking the time to talk to me about blackouts, and my friends Kevin and Alana Gallagher who put me in touch with them.

For my dear friends Michelene and Jack Toomey
With love

July 14th, 9 p.m.

1

A burst of humid air greeted Lorraine Lily as she exited the baggage claim area at Kennedy Airport and headed to the taxi stand. The unbearably hot night did nothing to improve her mood. Her high heels were killing her feet and she was tired. When she finally made it to the front of the line, the next yellow cab pulled up quickly. The driver popped the trunk, got out, and eyed her one carry-on bag.

"That's it?" he asked.

"They lost my luggage."

"What a surprise," he grunted. "Don't worry. In this weather, all you need is a bathing suit. Hop in."

In the back of the cab, Lorraine was grateful to find that at least the air-conditioning was functioning at a decent level. She pushed her auburn hair off her forehead and sighed. The driver looked at her through the rearview mirror.

"Where are you going?"

"Downtown Manhattan." She gave him the address. His only reaction was to step on the gas.

Lorraine reached into her massive handbag, pulled out her cell phone, and took a deep breath. How many more deep breaths am I going to need in my life? she wondered. She was sick of people telling her to take a deep breath. Everyone from the baggage claims supervisor to her estranged husband, Conrad. She'd had a wonderful three months away, and now it was back to reality.

P. Conrad Spreckles picked up on the second ring.

"I've landed," she told him.

"Back on home soil," he responded in a remote tone.

"They lost my luggage."

"It's probably wandering the earth. Just like its owner."

"I wasn't wandering the earth, dear. I was acting in an important new play that could be a springboard for my career."

"In a remote town in England with a population of eleven people. You may as well have performed it in our basement up here in Greenwich."

"We had wonderful audiences," Lorraine protested. "You wouldn't know since you didn't bother to come. Listen, Conrad, we need to talk. But right now I'm too tired. I'll sleep at the loft and take a car to Connecticut in the morning."

"There's nothing to talk about," he said flatly. "I filed for divorce."

Lorraine gasped. She was shocked that he'd taken such a drastic step. Not that she wanted to stay married. But she was hoping to be supported for a while longer while she pursued her career. Doing her best to sound saddened, she murmured. "Well, Conrad, if that's how you feel . . ."

"It's how I feel."

"Okay. I'll spend the night at the apartment . . ."

"You can't."

"Why not?"

"I sold it."

"You sold it?" Lorraine shrieked. The cabbie turned around to take a quick look, then shifted his attention back to the road. She lowered her voice and hissed, "How could you?"

"Funny you took the news very well about parting ways with me. But the thought of losing the apartment . . ."

"You had no right."

"I had every right. The loft was mine. It says so very clearly in the prenuptial agreement you signed two years ago." Conrad laughed mirthlessly. "That was when I believed you loved me for *me* instead of my money."

"I did love you . . ." Lorraine protested. "I mean I DO love you."

"Serves me right for letting my head be turned by a beautiful woman more than twenty years younger. Anyway, time to move on. I'll sell the house—the love nest we were going to be so happy in for the rest of our lives—and you'll get half."

Lorraine felt physically ill. "Who did you sell the loft to?" she sputtered.

"Our next-door neighbor Jack Reilly and his new wife, Regan. When they returned from their honeymoon three months ago, I made them an offer they couldn't refuse. They're already in the process of combining the two apartments. I'm sure they'll find a lot more happiness within those walls than we ever did. Although I suspect you might have experienced more happiness there than I ever knew about."

"That's not true!" Lorraine cried. "I only went there to rehearse scenes with my acting partners or have an occasional yoga session. I needed that apartment for my creativity and my alone time."

"I understand they have wonderful rehearsal space for rent at Carnegie Hall. Tonight you can come up here and stay in the guest room, or you can check into a hotel—your decision. You'll be hearing from my lawyer."

He hung up.

Lorraine's head was reeling. Jack Reilly was a cop. His wife was an investigator. If they discovered the safe she had installed behind the built-in cabinet in the closet, her life would be ruined. *I have to get in there again and soon,* she thought frantically. But how? She dug through her bag for her address book. She would call the young actor she'd rehearsed with in the loft not long before she left the States. Lorraine knew he needed money. She could tell he was the type who would help her if the price was right. Riffling through the pages, she located his number and began to dial.

Regan and Jack Reilly were driving south on Manhattan's West Side Highway, returning home from a three-day weekend on Cape Cod with Jack's family. It had been his father's birthday, and the clan had gathered to celebrate.

"We're almost there," Jack said with relief. "I thought coming back on a Monday, we'd beat some of the traffic. I wish we could have stayed longer, especially with this heat . . ."

"Me, too," Regan agreed. "But if the contractor actually shows up tomorrow, it'll be worth sweating it out. He swore to me he'd be there. We'll see."

"You're not sorry we got into all this are you?"

"Not at all. I love having a shopping cart full of contractor's supplies parked outside our bedroom." Regan smiled. "For years I've listened to my mother lament about how she and my father should have bought the apartment next door to theirs when it went up for sale. We got that chance and had to take it. When this renovation is finished, we'll have a home we'll never want to leave . . . if by then we haven't gone crazy."

Jack rolled his eyes. "Let's hope not." Five minutes later he was turning onto their block. "How about if I drop you off with the bags and then go get us some Chinese food? I also want to swing by the office and pick up a report."

"Sounds good. I'll open a bottle of wine and set the table on that new rooftop terrace of ours. It might not be in the best condition yet, but there should be at least a slight breeze coming off the Hudson."

They unloaded the car and placed the bags on a luggage cart. Regan brought the cart up to the loft Jack had purchased a couple of years before they met.

Inside the apartment, Regan turned on all the lights. The smell of plywood and sawdust filled the air. She wandered down the hallway to their "new" apartment and smiled.

What a mess, she thought as she looked at all the cans and nails and wood and debris. Hard to believe that this is really going to turn into something beautiful. I'd better open the door to the terrace and get some air in here, she thought. She walked to the corner of the spacious living/dining room and started up the spiral staircase toward the roof. She stopped for a moment. What was that noise she heard?

Nothing, she decided.

Regan tightened her grip on the railing and glanced out the window at the neighboring buildings. Feeling reassured by the familiar view she started up again. On the top step, she reached for the handle of the metal door that led to the terrace, then froze in place.

All of the lights had gone out.

Regan was standing alone in the pitch dark.

New York City had just been hit by a blackout.

2

At Larry's Laughs, a hot, cramped comedy club in Midtown Manhattan, Regan's best friend, Kit, was sitting at a table close to the small stage with a woman she had met just hours earlier. They were both attending a three-day insurance conference at the Gates Hotel on West Forty-fourth Street. Kit's crutches, her constant companions since foot surgery two weeks earlier, were on the floor next to her.

"After those dry-as-dust seminars, I could use a few laughs," Georgina had said to Kit during the cocktail and buffet reception. "It looks like you could, too. One of the bellmen told me there's a new comedy club not far from here. I'm trying to get a group together to leave this shindig as soon as the head of the conference makes his speech and it's safe for us to make our escape." She rolled her eyes and pretended to yawn. "How about it?"

Kit laughed. "If we can get a cab and the place is air-conditioned, I'm game," she said jovially, thinking it sounded like a good idea. Apparently no one else did. It ended up being just the two of them heading out for a taste of New York City nightlife.

Within minutes, Kit realized that she and Georgina were not on the path to a long and beautiful friendship. Georgina never stopped talking during the short cab ride to the club, swatting Kit's arm for emphasis every time she made a point. Her electric blue eyes darted around the cab, occasionally fixating on Kit with a disconcerting stare before turning away again. Kit learned that Georgina was single, hated her job, and was trying very hard to quit smoking. Attractive in an offbeat way, she was tall with long, brassy brown hair streaked with wide blond highlights, long bangs, and interesting features. Funky jewelry accessorized her simple, black summer sheath. Her long bronze nails matched her hair.

As they sat waiting for the show to start, a fidgety Georgina downed her margarita and then grabbed her purse off the floor. "I hope you don't mind, but I really need a smoke. I'll be right back."

"Not at all," Kit began, "but I think they're about to start the show—"

Georgina hadn't waited for a response. She was already heading for the door, squeezing her way through the tables that were crammed together.

Kit sighed. When nobody else wanted to join us, I should have just gone up to my room and watched a movie, she thought, suddenly aware that she was exhausted. Her foot started to ache. She longed to be back at the hotel, stretched out on her bed. Oh well, at least tomorrow night I'll be with Regan and Jack. She hadn't seen them since Memorial Day weekend when they'd been at Regan's parents' beach house in the Hamptons and gone through hundreds of wedding photos, dissecting every moment of Regan and Jack's big day.

Kit had had a great time at the reception even though she hadn't met anyone special. The one friend of Jack's Regan really wanted to introduce her to had called the morning of the wedding to say he couldn't make it. A girl he'd just started dating had been in a minor car accident and called him from the emergency room. He was on his way there. Turns out the damsel in distress had a couple of bruises and a fat lip that she milked for all it was worth. Now they were engaged. Just my luck, Kit thought, glancing around and checking out the crowd. I don't think there's anyone here who wants to fall in love with me while I recover from a bunionectomy. She then eyed the stage. Sitting this close to the action can be dangerous in a comedy club, she thought. But she'd been seated there to keep her sore foot out of harm's way.

Minutes passed. Where is Georgina? Kit wondered. Finally a spotlight started bouncing around the room, and a voice came over the loudspeaker. "Ladies and gentlemen, please turn off your cell phones, pagers, BlackBerries, and anything else that's sure to annoy your fellow man. And now, please welcome to Larry's Laughs, straight from Paramus, New Jersey, Mr. Billy Peebler!"

The audience applauded as a cute twenty-something guy with dark, curly hair ran onto the stage with great enthusiasm. Clad in jeans, sneakers, and a black T-shirt, he had a boyish charm. His brown eyes were twinkling, and he was smiling broadly, but Kit got the feeling he was slightly nervous. Who wouldn't be? she thought. Coming out onto a bare stage to tell jokes takes a lot of guts.

"Hey, everybody," Billy called out. "Good to see you." He pulled the microphone out of the stand, held it in his hands, and paused.

"Tell a joke!" a guy in the back yelled.

"Give me a chance, buddy!" Billy answered with a smile. "Have you ever heard of comic timing?"

"I've never heard of you!" the heckler answered loudly.

Billy ignored him. "You know it's so hot out there, this afternoon I stopped for a nice cold one in my neighborhood pub. I was sitting there minding my own business when a horse wandered in. The bartender says to him, 'Why the long face?' "

Kit chuckled as did most of the audience. As Billy paused, even more of them laughed.

"You know what the horse said?" Billy finally asked.

"I don't care!" the heckler yelled.

A now irritated Kit turned in the direction of the heckler and shouted, "Be quiet!"

Billy looked down at her and smiled. "Did my mother send you here tonight?"

Before Kit could answer, the spotlight went out.

"Someone was smart enough to pull the plug!" the heckler yelled in the room now dimly lit by just the small candles on each table. The whir of the air conditioner stopped, groaned, and sputtered to a halt.

"There's been a blackout!" someone cried from the doorway to the bar area.

"A blackout!"

"Oh no!"

"Let's get out of here!"

"I have to get home!"

People quickly jumped up, some accidentally knocking their chairs into each other. The darkened room suddenly felt stifling. Within seconds there was near pandemonium as waiters tried to collect money for the drinks and patrons were crowding the exit.

I guess it's a good thing I sat up front, Kit thought. My foot definitely would have been trampled if I were in the middle of this bedlam. I'll just wait here for a few minutes. With any luck Georgina will be outside and we'll manage to find a cab.

"Are you okay?"

Kit turned. Billy Peebler was standing next to her. "Oh hello . . . ," she said.

He smiled at her. "Hello, yourself. Thanks for speaking up for me."

"That guy was a jerk."

"I know. But in this business you have to expect it."

"I can't believe a blackout hit when you were onstage."

"I'm thrilled. I think I was about to bomb. I could feel it in my bones."

Kit smiled. "No you weren't. Your first joke was funny."

"It's one of the oldest jokes in the book, but it's just silly enough to get that first laugh. What are you doing here by yourself?"

"The person I came with went out for a smoke . . ."

"Now that sounds like the beginning of a joke."

Kit smiled and made a face. "I wish it were."

They spoke for a few minutes while the room cleared. When everyone was out, it had a lonely, abandoned feeling. Only a few candles were still flickering.

"Let's see if we can find your friend," Billy said. He quickly pushed the overturned chairs out of the way, then carefully escorted Kit out to the sidewalk, his arm around her shoulder. The streets were dark, horns were honking in the distance, there was a sense of excitement in the air. But no sign of Georgina.

"I can't believe it!" Kit said, shaking her head. "I'm hobbling on crutches, and she disappears. And she's the one who invited me here tonight."

The hostess who had seated Kit and Georgina was standing by the doorway. "Are you looking for the girl you came in with?"

"Yes."

"I saw her out here smoking. Some tall, cute guy with blond hair bummed a cigarette off of her. A few minutes later they got in a cab. I thought to myself—'That was fast!'"

"What?" Kit asked with astonishment. "She actually left me here like this? That's swell." Kit looked at Billy and smiled. "I can tell you one thing. If I have anything to do with it, her name is going to be mud in the insurance industry. Come to think of it, I don't even know her last name. I don't even have her cell phone number to call. Wait until I run into her tomorrow . . ."

"I'll get you home," Billy said. "Where do you live?"

"Hartford."

"Oh . . ."

" 'Oh' is right. I'm staying on the thirty-eighth floor of the Gates Hotel, so that's not going to work, either.

I don't think I have the energy to hop up that many flights on one foot. My best friend lives downtown in Tribeca. I'll give her a call and see if she's home. She has a fourth-floor loft that I think I can manage. I just hope she's there . . ."

3

Jack was over at One Police Plaza within minutes of leaving Regan. One of the reasons he'd bought an apartment in Tribeca was so he'd be close to the office. His wasn't a nine to five existence—he could be called in at any time, day or night, when a case was breaking. Jack didn't mind; he loved his work. After graduating from Boston College, he'd decided to pursue a career in law enforcement. He'd risen through the ranks of the New York Police Department from patrolman to captain and a few years later he became the head of the Major Case Squad. His goal was to one day be police commissioner. Now that he'd found Regan, Jack felt his whole life had fallen into place.

People remarked on what a handsome couple they made. Thirty-four-year-old Jack was six-feet-two-inches tall with broad shoulders, sandy hair, and even features. Thirty-one-year-old Regan was five foot seven and one of the Black Irish. She had dark hair, blue eyes, and a fair complexion. They looked like they were made for each other.

"I wish I'd met you years ago," he often told her.

"Me, too, Jack. Believe me! But now we really appreciate each other," she'd answer with a smile and a raised eyebrow.

Things were so good, it sometimes worried him. But as Regan always said, worrying was part of being Irish. He smiled at the memory of her playful teasing, parked his car, and got out. Ah, life is grand, he thought, even if it feels like 110 degrees in this city tonight.

He hurried into the building, greeted the guard, and took the elevator up to his office. Ducking into a hallway bathroom, he washed his hands and splashed cool water on his face. This doesn't feel as refreshing as the water of Cape Cod Bay, he thought. It was hard to believe he and Regan had been taking a cool dip at the beach behind his parents' house just this morning. After the long trip home, that refreshing swim seemed like ages ago.

Down the hall, two of his detectives were talking animatedly on their phones in the outer room of the Major Case Squad. As soon as Jack walked through the door, he could sense that something big was going on. Joe Azzolino looked up, covered the phone with his hand, and called out, "You're not supposed to be here. I guess you're psychic."

"What are you talking about?" Jack asked.

Joe looked surprised. "You haven't heard?"

"Heard what?" Jack asked, trying not to sound impatient.

"New York City is in a blackout. So is New Jersey and Connecticut and parts of the Midwest."

"As of when?"

"Three or four minutes ago."

Because One Police Plaza had its own generator, it wouldn't be immediately apparent to everyone in the building.

"Do we know what caused it?" Jack asked quickly.

"There's a thunderstorm in the Midwest. A lightning strike in Ohio knocked out their grids and started a cascading failure. Which is good news. Con Ed just put out the word that it's not sabotage or terrorism."

"Thank God," Jack said quietly. He exhaled hard and hurried into his office. So much for a relaxing night on the roof deck eating Chinese food, he thought as he quickly dialed Regan on their home phone. He let it ring and ring but there was no answer. With the power out, the answering machine didn't work. His heart skipped a beat as the empty sound of the ringing phone filled his ear. He hung up and dialed Regan's cell phone. That rang until her voice mail picked up. "Regan, it's me. Where are you?" he asked uneasily. "Give me a call." He hung up the phone. By now she should have gotten the flashlight out of the drawer in the kitchen, he thought. If she left the apartment, she would have taken her cell phone. He tried the home number again, letting it ring a dozen times. Nothing.

Quickly he strode back into the outer room. "I just dropped Regan off at the apartment and she's not answering the phone—I'll be right back—you know what to do—I have my cell phone."

He was gone.

• • •

Standing on the top step in the pitch darkness, Regan's heart was beating fast. What happened? she wondered. Is this a blackout? Quickly she debated whether to navigate her way through the debris downstairs and look for a flashlight or go out on the roof and hope the candle they left on the table last week would still be there. She knew that one of the construction guys went out on the roof to smoke. She had seen a cigarette lighter on the table . . . and outside there should be at least some light from the sky.

She opted for the great outdoors. Regan turned the handle, pushed the creaky metal door outward, and carefully stepped down onto the terrace. It was immediately apparent that New York City was in the dark. She looked west and could tell that New Jersey had also been affected. The high-rises overlooking the Hudson River had disappeared into the vast blackness.

Her eyes hungrily absorbing whatever light there was, Regan leaned down and felt around on the ground for the piece of wood they used to keep the door propped open. It was right at her feet. Curling her fingers around the temporary doorstop, she wedged it into the two-inch space between the metal frame and the cement roof. I can't wait to replace this door, she thought, and put in a good alarm system. A little fake grass wouldn't hurt, either.

She stood up straight in the dark. Everything was eerily silent. She and Jack lived in a quiet neighborhood, but now it felt like a ghost town. Carefully,

Regan walked over to the rickety table where they'd planned to dine this evening. The candle in the red jar with the white netting was where they left it. Score one, she thought as she picked it up.

Behind her the creaky metal door snapped shut. Regan spun around. She ran over and tried to open it but it was locked. The wedge was nowhere on the ground. This door was closed deliberately, she thought. Someone is in the apartment. They must have made the noise I heard.

Regan knew if she started yelling she'd risk the intruder coming back to shut her up, and she had nothing to use as a weapon except the candle. Let them take what they want, she thought. Her heart was pounding as she pushed herself back against the wall behind the door, ready to spring, in case the night visitor decided to reappear.

Jack was back in his car and racing through the darkened streets as fast as he felt was safe. The traffic lights were out and already there were citizens at the intersections directing traffic. He kept trying to reach Regan, but to no avail. He called their neighbor who lived below them, but she didn't answer either.

This doesn't make sense, he thought. Regan would have called me by now if she were okay.

When he reached their building, he grabbed the flashlight he kept in the glove compartment and jumped out of the car. Another neighbor was coming out the door.

"Jack!" she said. "I was just walking down the stairs in the dark. A guy came running from behind and almost knocked me over. I'm sure he doesn't live here—"

Jack sailed past her. He raced up the four flights of stairs to their apartment, taking the steps two at a time. He unlocked the door and hurried inside.

"Regan!" he called frantically, pointing the flashlight around the room. "Regan!"

No answer. He ran through the rooms looking for her. In their new loft, construction debris was all over the floor.

"Regan!" he called, kicking a piece of plywood out of his way. He shone the flashlight around the room, then raced up the steps to the roof. "Regan!" he called as he pushed the door open.

Behind the door Regan dropped the candle that she had poised over her head, ready to strike, and flew into his arms. "Jack!"

"What am I going to do with you?" he asked, his voice husky, as he held her tight.

"We had an unexpected guest."

"I heard."

After a moment, Regan looked up at him and smiled. "What, no Chinese food?"

4

Sitting in the back of the cab as it sped toward Manhattan, Lorraine Lily was at her wit's end. Hot, tired, jet-lagged, and fearful, she'd left a message for Clay Nardellini, her fellow actor, on his cell phone. She hoped he hadn't gotten a part that had taken him out of town. That would be awful.

Lorraine didn't know what to do next. She hadn't even told the driver yet that her destination had changed. There was no way she was going to give Conrad the satisfaction of showing up in Connecticut looking for shelter. How could he have sold the loft behind my back? she thought furiously. She quivered at the thought of what she'd left in the safe.

I wish I could just turn around and get on the next plane back to England. All her joy at being praised by the British critics as a "sexy, interesting actress to keep an eye on," had evaporated. On the plane, she'd been thinking up witty things she'd say, little stories she could tell when she finally was asked to be a guest on the late-night talk shows. She was imagining all the things she would do when she was famous. Now, just a few hours later, she was without her luggage and wondering where she was going to spend the night.

I'm going to have to get a hotel room, she thought. I need to take a shower and I need to be in the city. I'm not leaving until I clear out that safe. If Clay doesn't call back, I'll have to figure out another plan. She closed her eyes and leaned her head back, thinking regretfully about the loft that she loved. Now those Reillys had their mitts on it. This couldn't be worse, she thought. It just couldn't. As the cab rumbled along, she pondered which hotel she should grace her presence with.

"Holy Toledo!" the cab driver blurted.

Lorraine opened her eyes, looked ahead, then lunged forward. They were approaching the Fifty-ninth Street Bridge. The silhouette of Manhattan was black and spooky. "Oh, my God!" she cried.

"I saw the whole thing!" the driver crowed as he fumbled to switch on the radio. "It's like someone flipped a switch. I hope it's nothing bad—"

An announcer's excited voice came through the rear speaker, loud and clear. Lorraine felt as if he were shouting in her ear. "The lights have just gone out all over the city—we will keep you updated with all the latest news . . ."

"I have to get a hotel room!" Lorraine cried.

"What?" the driver asked, begrudgingly lowering the volume.

"I have to check into a hotel!"

"A hotel?"

"Yes. It's a long and sad story."

"We've all got problems, lady. Let me tell you something, you're not going to have much luck getting a hotel room now. The city is packed with tourists and business people attending conventions. Some of them are probably stuck on elevators as we speak. Others won't be able to get up to their rooms. Finding a room at all, never mind one on a low floor, will be like finding a needle in a haystack."

"But I have to!"

"Just tell me where you want me to drop you off. I'm not a travel agent."

Lorraine pulled out her cell phone. She tried to dial information but all the circuits were busy. "Ohhh. My life is falling apart."

"Lady, we're getting close to the other side of this bridge. You gotta tell me where to go. Driving through town in the dark with no traffic lights is not my idea of fun." He paused. "But who knows? Maybe I'll make some extra bucks tonight. People will be desperate for cabs. So where to?"

"The Sapphire."

"Fancy shmancy," the driver muttered under his breath.

They slowly crossed into a darkened Manhattan. Cars were hesitantly crawling through the streets. People were pouring out of restaurants. Headlights from the cars provided the only source of light. It was like they were in a movie, but Lorraine wasn't paying much attention. She was busy reapplying her lipstick and carefully touching up her face, aided only by the light of her compact. It was something she could have done in her sleep.

The driver had turned up the volume of the radio again and listened to the reports. "Can you imagine that?" he asked Lorraine, not expecting an answer. "A lightning strike leads to this mess."

When they finally pulled up to the Sapphire, the doorman waved them on. "I wouldn't bother. They're all booked up. It's chaos in there," he said with a bored expression.

Lorraine squealed in despair.

"Shhhhh," the driver said, as he cocked his head toward the radio. "Listen—"

". . . yes, that's right, folks. We just got word that the Treetops Hotel on Central Park South, which was scheduled for a grand opening in two days, is opening its doors tonight. Employees were there making final preparations for its first guests. Now you could be one of them! The manager claims they want to come to the aid of the citizens of New York. Those citizens who can cough up at least a thousand dollars a room. But they have a state-of-the-art generator that is sure to cool your jets . . ."

"Take me there!" Lorraine cried.

"You're going to pay that much for a room?" the driver asked incredulously.

"My soon-to-be-ex-husband will foot the bill."

"I better get a good tip."

Fifteen minutes later the cab pulled up to the marbled entrance of the Treetops. There was already a line at the registration desk in the lobby. A local TV reporter with a camera crew was covering the story of the luxury hotel welcoming hot and tired victims of the blackout. Lorraine was only too happy to be interviewed. The sight of a camera temporarily took her mind off her problems.

"I just returned from doing a play in London," she cooed. "I feel as if I'm in a play right now. The airlines lost my luggage—"

"They lost your luggage?" the young reporter asked with great interest.

Lorraine laughed and tossed her head back. "Can you imagine? I'm telling you, it's all just too much . . ."

By the time Lorraine finished talking about her luggage and her exciting life as an actress, there were no rooms left. Just two suites. At four thousand dollars a pop.

"What?" she gulped to the clerk.

"If you hadn't posed for the camera I would have had a nice cozy room for you for twelve hundred. But look at it on the bright side. The suite faces the park. The room faces an alley."

"You can't see anything out there no matter which direction you face."

"Take it or leave it."

Lorraine slapped Conrad's credit card onto the granite counter just as her cell phone began to ring. Clay Nardellini was calling back. And he was only three blocks away.

31

5

Regan and Jack retrieved a second flashlight from their kitchen drawer and methodically started to look around the apartment. Their bedroom, the place where most thieves would head immediately, seemed untouched. The safe that was bolted to the floor of their closet was still locked. Jack quickly opened it and saw that the contents were undisturbed. Regan's jewelry, their passports, papers, and extra cash seemed to all be the way they had left them.

"He couldn't have been here long if he didn't touch this," Jack observed.

The second bedroom was also undisturbed. Aside from some construction materials, nothing in their original loft looked out of place.

They walked back down the hall to their new apartment, which they sometimes referred to as "Lorraine's Lair" or simply "the Lair." Over the past two years, Jack had noticed that it was only she who seemed to spend any time there. Different guys had come in and out, and she always introduced them as fellow students in her acting class. There was never any sign of Conrad, but when he sold the loft to them, there was no sign of Lorraine.

The construction crew had started their renovation on the Lair, and just last week had broken down the wall between the two apartments. There was no sign of forced entry at either front door. There was also no sign of forced entry at the door to the roof.

"When we left here Thursday night everything was locked up tight," Jack said. "Rod and his guys weren't supposed to come in when we were gone, were they?"

"He told me if they got in supplies they might drop them off," Regan said as she shone her flashlight around, then walked over and opened the large front closet. Last time she looked, the closet had been empty. Now several boxes of expensive Italian tile were piled high against the wall. "I guess Rod was here. The good news is that the tile they told us would take six months for delivery has arrived. The bad news is that they might have accidentally left the door unlocked. I know when they're hauling stuff out to the service elevator they push in the button of the door so it doesn't lock. Either that or someone who has a key came in here tonight."

"His crew knew we were going away," Jack commented. "Why would any of them wait until the night we're due back to wander in? That doesn't make sense. But who else would?" Jack shook his head. "Of course we never had the locks changed when we bought the apartment because it didn't matter yet. There was nothing to steal and the wall to our place hadn't been knocked down. The construction people would be coming in and out anyway." He sighed. "Who knows how many people who worked for Conrad and Lorraine had keys to this place? Tomorrow morning we've got to get a locksmith in here."

The two of them stood in the dark, their flashlights facing the floor. "The intruder could have just run away when I was on the roof," Regan said. "After he locked me out, he must have been looking around to make sure he didn't forget anything he brought in with him."

"He was probably also afraid that the lights would come back on and you'd get a look at him."

They carefully shone their flashlights around the room. "That tile is nice with the hand-painted pictures of jugs of wine, loaves of bread, and scenes from Tuscany, but I don't think it's worth risking jail time for," Regan said sardonically. "There's nothing else back here. Conrad might have given us a good price, but he made sure this place was stripped. There wasn't a picture hook left on the walls—" She stopped talking when her flashlight revealed a small dark object on the floor, slightly hidden by a piece of wood. It was just a few steps from the front door. Jack saw it, too. He walked over, leaned down, picked it up, and held it out in front of them.

They both were silent as they realized what they were looking at.

A lightning-rod stun gun that resembled a pen. With a built-in flashlight.

Regan swallowed. "He's really going to be mad he lost it, now that we're in a blackout . . ."

Jack didn't laugh. "If he'd zapped you with this, you could have been badly hurt. Come on. I want to put this in a plastic bag."

They headed to the kitchen where Regan's purse was sitting on the counter next to their Imus mugs. Her cell phone started to ring.

"There's a message from me on there," Jack said as he pulled open a drawer. "I have to go back to the office but I'm not leaving you here alone."

"Is it Bring Your Wife to Work night?" Regan asked lightly as she retrieved the phone. It was Kit.

"Regan, you're not going to believe what happened."

Regan smiled. "Oh, yes, I would."

"No, really. This is a first—a woman I met at the convention left me stranded at a comedy club. I'm stuck here in Midtown and, as you know, I'm on crutches. My hotel room is on the thirty-eighth floor. It's impossible to get a cab. Luckily I'm with this nice comedian who is looking after me. Could you come and get me and bring me to your place?"

"Our apartment isn't so appealing these days, either," Regan said. "For a lot of reasons. But of course I'll come and get you. It might take a few minutes with the traffic lights all out."

"I'm not going anywhere. My new friend, Billy, and I are sitting here on someone's front stoop on Fifty-fourth Street between Ninth and Tenth Avenues. People are coming out of their apartments with folding chairs and bottles of beer and wine. One guy said it's about time they had a block party."

"Save me a seat," Regan joked as she took down the exact address. When she hung up, Jack turned to her.

He'd been examining the stun gun through a plastic bag.

"You're picking up Kit?"

"At least you don't have to worry about me being alone."

"She's on crutches. Our intruder wouldn't need a stun gun to fight her off."

"You never know with Kit. Don't worry. We'll be fine."

"I wish I didn't have to go back to the office. But on a night like tonight . . ."

Now it was Jack's cell phone that rang. Keith Waters, his top assistant, was calling.

"Jack, a new gallery in SoHo has been burglarized. They broke in the back door and stole glass sculptures worth several hundred thousand dollars. With the power out, the alarm didn't work. The owners ran over from their apartment as soon as the blackout struck. It was too late—"

"What's the address?" Jack asked quickly. When he hung up, he took Regan's hand. "Let's get out of here. I'll take you down to your car. Promise me that no matter what happens you won't come back here alone."

"Jack, don't worry, I won't. Even if the lights go back on, I'll bring Kit back here."

"We should be so lucky," Jack said. "I have the feeling this is going to be a long night."

6

Conrad Spreckles was relaxing in the tastefully
appointed den of his Greenwich home, suffering no dis-
comfort from the blackout that had affected so many
people in the tristate area and beyond. He was cooled
not only by the power of his own private generator, but
also the vodka on ice that he held in his hands.

He felt great satisfaction at having broken the news
to Lorraine that the loft was sold. Taking a gentle sip
of his drink, he relished the thought of her displeasure.
He wished he could have told her in person and seen
the look on her face, but he had no choice—it would
have been embarrassing if she'd gone to the loft
tonight and tried to get in. The Reillys didn't need to
know about their personal problems. At the closing
they'd asked him about Lorraine. He'd informed them
that she was in England acting in a play. He could tell
they found the situation a little curious, but they were
polite and didn't probe. If only his first ex-wife would
behave with such grace.

Penny was reveling in his misery. They had been
married for twenty-five years when he met Lorraine.
When Conrad told Penny he wanted a divorce, he'd
insisted it didn't have to do with anyone else. But it
eventually came out that indeed he had met and
courted Lorraine when he was still married. Penny
and his twenty-year-old daughter, Alexis, his little

princess, would never forgive him. He knew that he had made the mistake of the century. So did everyone in Darien where Penny still lived. Soon everyone in Greenwich would realize, too.

He'd been made a fool of. The young, sexy actress had only been after him for his money. The money the Spreckles family had made after years of selling quality chocolates around the world. His grandparents had started the business at the stove of their tiny apartment in the Bronx. His father had built up the company, and Conrad and his brother had taken it global. The Spreckles name was synonymous with gourmet chocolates no one in the universe could resist.

Conrad took another sip of his drink and stared at the television. The station he was watching was covering the blackout. He expected Lorraine to come through the door at any minute. What else could she do? New York City was in chaos. When he saw her face on the screen, he jumped out of his chair and ran closer to his sixty-inch flat-screen TV. There she was in high definition, looking as beautiful as ever.

"I was just in a play—" she cooed.

"That little—" he spat. She was checking in to that exorbitantly expensive hotel! With his money! She didn't look like a woman whose husband had just told her he had filed for divorce. Conrad grabbed the vodka bottle and refilled his glass.

I'm going to get my revenge! he thought. She is going to be sorry. I don't know how I'm going to do it, but I have to figure out something.

The phone rang. The second he picked it up he realized he'd made a mistake. Penny, sitting in her generator-cooled house, was on the line.

"Hello, dear," she said sweetly. "If you're not watching, you must turn on the news . . ."

7

At the wheel of her Lexus, Regan drove carefully through the darkened streets of Manhattan. Heading uptown on Tenth Avenue, she was half listening to the radio reports on the blackout. Her mind kept going back to what had just happened at the apartment. To think that someone had been in there when she arrived. Someone with a stun gun. I was lucky, she thought. Really lucky.

Who could it have been? Regan wondered as she drove. Could it have been someone from the construction crew? She didn't think so but she did find one of the guys a bit surly and unfriendly. That doesn't make him a criminal, she reminded herself. Well, whoever it was must have been thrilled that the blackout struck and they could make their escape without being seen and possibly identified. They won't be nearly as thrilled when they realize they dropped their weapon.

Jack had taken the stun gun with him to have it tested for prints and see if they could trace the owner.

Regan sighed. Her mother had been concerned that

she was moving into a nondoorman building. "I'm not worried about when you're with Jack . . . It's just when you go up to the apartment alone."

As if on cue, Regan's cell phone, which she'd programmed into the car radio, started to ring. Nora Regan Reilly, best-selling suspense writer, and Regan's father, Luke, owner of three funeral homes in New Jersey, were in Los Angeles to meet with a producer about a television deal for several of Nora's books. Regan pushed the OK button and answered. Her mother's voice came through the car's speakers.

"Regan, we just got out of a screening and heard about the blackout. Are you all right?"

"I'm fine," Regan answered.

"Are you sure? Where are you?"

"I'm in the car on my way to pick up Kit. She's still on crutches, and walking up to her thirty-eighth-floor hotel room isn't an option."

"You're driving around? Be careful. The traffic lights must be out!"

Regan smiled. "That they are." This is definitely not the time to tell her about the break-in, Regan thought. There's no use worrying her even more. "I'm going to pick up Kit and head back home. Who'd have guessed that all those candlesticks we received as wedding presents would come in so handy this soon?"

"Be careful of setting the place on fire."

"I'll do my best."

"Where's Jack?"

"He'll be working all night tonight. Someone

already broke into an art gallery in SoHo."

"Oh dear, there wasn't too much crime or looting during the last blackout in New York," Nora said.

"That struck in the afternoon. People had time to take measures to guard their businesses before it got dark. When it happens at night and everything gets thrown into darkness so fast, people who ordinarily wouldn't steal can act impulsively. . . ." What am I saying this to my mother for, Regan wondered. "But on the radio they're saying that things are pretty peaceful so far. It's well past rush hour, so most of the commuters have already left the city."

"Get home as soon as you can and lock the doors."

"I will. Say hi to Dad. I'll talk to you tomorrow."

At Fifty-fourth Street, Regan turned right. Her headlights shone onto a block party in full swing. Music was blaring, people were dancing in the street, and flames were lapping from barbecue grills that had been carted out onto the sidewalk. Regan inched her way forward, on the lookout for the address Kit had given her. She knew it was on the right hand side of the street. Glancing around, Regan thought it could have been New Year's Eve. All the stoops were overflowing with revelers. Everyone on this block must have invited their friends over. Finally she double-parked the car and got out.

"Regan!" Kit called through the crowd, crutching her way toward the car. A young guy was clearing the path for her.

Regan hurried over to open the passenger door. She

hugged Kit, who she could tell was tense. Her foot must really be hurting, Regan thought.

"Regan, this is Billy," Kit said brusquely. "He's coming with us."

"Sure," Regan answered, as she shook Billy's hand, hoping he wasn't some nutcase. But he looked and seemed like a sweet guy.

While Kit maneuvered herself into the front seat, Billy got in the back, and Regan threw the crutches in the trunk.

When they were all in the car, Regan joked, "This party looks like fun. Are you sure you want to leave? Those hot dogs smell good."

Kit put her hand on Regan's arm. "Regan—" she began, then paused.

"Kit, what's wrong? Do you feel all right?"

"I just got a phone call from someone at the conference who's over at the hotel and knew I went to a comedy club with that girl—"

"The one who left you there."

Kit nodded. "Georgina Mathieson is her name. A good friend of hers was arrested today for shoplifting. She and Georgina went on quite a spree in Atlanta on Saturday. Someone wrote down part of this other girl's license plate number. They have the two of them on security tapes, stuffing clothing into their bags. The police caught up with Georgina's friend Paulette a few hours ago."

"Georgina's a shoplifter?" Regan asked. "Maybe she's headed down to my apartment."

"What?"

"Someone broke in tonight. I walked in on them and they got away."

"That's terrible!" Kit said. "But, Regan, this is worse!"

Regan was about to make a flippant remark, but Kit looked so worried, she stopped herself. "Tell me."

"This Paulette is cooperating with the police. She told them that Georgina picks up blond guys in comedy clubs, drugs them with knockout drops, then lures them to her car and drives to an isolated place where she burns their arm with a brand that says I AM A SNAKE and leaves them there. Just like she left me tonight! After spending a few minutes with her, I could tell she was odd, but not this crazy. Regan, the hostess at the comedy club said earlier that she'd seen Georgina smoking out on the sidewalk, then getting into a cab with a guy who bummed a cigarette from her. A guy who's blond! He doesn't know what he's in for!"

"Comedy clubs!" Billy practically squeaked from the back seat. "My parents never wanted me to be a comedian. Wait until they hear this! For once I'm glad I don't have blond hair."

"Kit, I wonder why she invited you to go out with her then."

"She'd been trying to get a group together. She doesn't have a car so maybe she didn't plan on attacking anyone tonight. But the opportunity arose and she couldn't resist."

"Is that hostess still at the club?" Regan asked.

"Yes," Billy answered. "I called. She said she'd wait there if you want to go over and talk to her."

"Of course I do," Regan said.

Outside the car, the music on the street was playing louder than ever. People were joyously joining in song. "I want to rock and roll all night . . ."

"This guy is going to be scarred for life if someone doesn't find them," Kit moaned. "Maybe even worse. If I hadn't agreed to go out with her tonight, she might not have met him . . ."

"It's not your fault, Kit," Regan said. "We'll do everything we can to find them. I'll call Jack and he'll get the word out. Of course, this isn't the best night to be trying to locate—"

"An assaultive wacko."

Regan turned the key in the ignition, pressed in Jack's number on her cell phone, and slowly steered the car through the throng of partyers. All thoughts of the attempted burglary at her apartment had disappeared.

"Kit, reach in my purse and get out my notebook," Regan instructed as Jack's cell phone began to ring. "Start writing down everything you remember about Georgina. Everything she said, everything she did. What she had to drink before she disappeared—"

"It was a margarita," Kit said as she opened Regan's purse, "with extra salt. She downed it in about two gulps."

Jack's voice came through the car speakers. From

his caller ID he knew it was Regan calling him. "Regan, are you all right?" he asked anxiously.

"I'm fine. I'm with Kit."

"Can I call you back? We're in the middle of—"

"No, Jack," Regan answered. "I'm quite sure you'll want to hear this right away . . ."

8

"This isn't a bad place to sit out the blackout," Clay Nardellini pronounced as, chewing on a toothpick, he strolled into Lorraine's suite. "You're staying cool up here in grand style while the rest of the city is fanning themselves with rolled up newspapers. The Candy Man must be selling lots of chocolates."

Lorraine rolled her eyes. "I needed a place to stay. Conrad sold the loft to our next-door neighbors while I was in England."

Clay's brown eyes widened. In his late twenties, he was five foot ten, with brown hair, olive skin, and a slightly stocky build. He was attractive but had a tough street quality, which meant that he was almost always cast to play a criminal. It was a source of frustration that he'd shared with his acting class. With the support of his teacher, Wendall, and his fellow students, he was working hard to develop his sensitive side. He was also taking speech lessons in an effort to sound more refined and dance classes to put some elegance in his swagger. His burning desire was to play a romantic lead opposite a hot young actress. "He sold it? You loved that place."

Lorraine shrugged. "You want a drink?"

"I'll take a beer."

Lorraine poured herself a glass of white wine from the open bottle on the table, then grabbed a bottle of beer out of the minibar. She walked over to the long, white overstuffed couch that faced Central Park. The whole suite was decorated in white, including the carpeting, walls, furniture, and knickknacks. The hotel's decorator was obviously a proponent of white's purity, which undoubtedly would end up driving the cleaning staff crazy. Lorraine handed Clay his drink, and they both sat.

Clay gratefully sipped the cold brew. "That tastes good. So Lorraine, to what do I owe this honor? You just got off a plane from England and you call me? Where's the Candy Man?"

Lorraine sat back, propping up a fluffy pillow behind her. "He filed for divorce."

"I'm sorry to hear that," Clay said tenderly, always at work on that sensitive streak.

"That's not my problem."

"It's not?"

"No." Lorraine curled her manicured toes around the plush, white carpeting. "Remember how Wendall told us that if we had a problem with someone we should write them a letter and tell them exactly how we feel?"

"Of course. Get everything off your chest in the

letter but never mail it. It's great therapy and a lot cheaper than paying a shrink."

Lorraine nodded. "I guess I really wanted to heal myself because I wrote letters to almost everyone in my life. Personal and professional. But then I carried it even further. Not only did I write to every casting director, producer, and director who hadn't hired me but I wrote nasty letters to everyone in the business, even people I hadn't met yet. I didn't mean what I wrote—some of the letters are pretty vicious—but I thought the whole exercise would make me feel more confident."

"Whoa!" Clay exclaimed. He shook his head in disbelief, then looked at her questioningly. "When did you have time to write all these letters? Oh wait, I forgot, you don't have to work to pay the rent." He paused. "Did you write one to me?"

"Do you think I'd be telling you this if I did?"

"I guess not. Why are you telling me now?"

Lorraine swallowed hard. "I had a safe installed in the loft that Conrad didn't know about. It's hidden behind a cabinet in the front closet. Those letters are in the safe. If someone finds them, I'm dead. My career is over."

"That's for sure," Clay said quickly. "People in our business hold grudges."

Lorraine winced.

Clay leaned forward. "Don't you think your neighbors will give the letters back? If they even find them?"

"They might mail them! I went so far as to address

the envelopes and put stamps on them. And if they did give them back, they'd give them to Conrad. He was the sole owner of the loft."

"You were really committed to this project, weren't you?"

"Wendall always told us to be committed to achieving our dream. So I was! But if Conrad gets his hands on those letters he'll read them, then run straight to the post office to mail them himself! I know he will."

"Is there a letter to him?"

Lorraine nodded. "It's ten pages long." She sighed and tightened her grip on her wine glass. "I handwrote every single letter in my beautiful penmanship. So I can't deny I wrote them. I have to get the letters back and I need your help."

"My help? I'm sick of playing criminals and now you're asking me to be one in real life. What was that commercial? 'I'm not a doctor but I play one on TV.' Well, I'm not a criminal even though I play one much too often!"

"This would be so easy for you. You work as a handyman on the side. You could figure out a way to get in the loft. I'm not asking you to steal anything that isn't mine. Those letters belong to me!"

"Is there any cash in the safe?"

"Yes, and it's all yours! I put some away here and there because Conrad could be so stingy. Somewhere between twenty and thirty thousand dollars. I'm not exactly sure how much."

Clay's jaw dropped. "You're not sure if it's twenty or thirty thousand dollars?"

"No, I'm not. If you do this for me, the money is all yours. Please, Clay, my whole career is at stake. I'm on my way to being famous—the British critics said so—and those letters would end it all."

"I could go on a game show and win at least twenty thousand dollars," Clay protested. "And I wouldn't be risking jail time."

"But you haven't, have you?" Lorraine asked. "Besides, most of them are taped in Los Angeles." On the coffee table, Lorraine's cell phone began to ring. Quickly she answered. It was Edwin, the producer of the play in England.

"Darling Lorraine, I couldn't sleep and turned on the telly. I understand it's a bit dark over there now. My goodness!"

"Yes, Edwin," Lorraine cooed. "We're coping as best as we can. Oh, how I already miss doing the play. It's as if I have a big hole in my heart. I feel such a sense of loss. I miss being with you and the cast—"

"You too, darling," Edwin interrupted. "Now listen, I was going to call you tomorrow anyway. My friend Charles, the director from Hollywood who came to the play on closing night, really found you to be a delightful actress—"

Lorraine's heart sank. Charles Dryden was a well-known, well-respected director. The letter she'd written to him had been particularly brutal. In it she'd said his films were unwatchable and she wouldn't be caught dead appearing in one.

"—he just signed on to direct a big important picture and he has a lovely role in it for you. I want you to call him in the morning . . ."

When Lorraine hung up the phone, she was on the verge of hysteria. "Clay, there is also valuable jewelry in the safe. You can have it all. I just want the letters. Please!"

Clay, knowing full well that the money he'd make in one night was a lot more than he'd make in a year of poking around people's apartments fixing their clogged sinks, placed his beer down on the table and paused. "All right, Lorraine, I'll do it. I wouldn't want to deprive the world of your talents."

Lorraine threw her arms around him. "Wendall said we worked well together. I know we can do it again!"

"This is reality, Lorraine," Clay said solemnly, "not a scene from class. If it doesn't work out we'll both end up behind bars at Riker's Island. And I do mean both of us. You're coming up with me to the apartment."

"Of course," Lorraine said. "We're in this together." Nervously she picked up her drink. No use telling him who owns the apartment, she thought. If he found out it was the head of the Major Case Squad, he'd never do it. No matter how much money was involved.

9

Back at Larry's Laughs, Regan, Kit, and Billy sat down at a candlelit table with Becky, the young hostess who had only been working there for two weeks. Just twenty-one, she was between her junior and senior year of college, and had been hired for the summer. Her red hair was pulled back in a ponytail, and she was wearing a short skirt and sleeveless top. She exuded a youthful exuberance and was clearly awed by the excitement. Billy made the introductions.

The room was so dark, it felt like a cave. But it was the only place where they could all sit together and talk. Becky's hostess stand was at the entrance to the back room, facing the front area with its small bar and big glass window overlooking the street.

"Becky, you know why we're here," Regan began.

Becky nodded. "I can't believe it."

"Can you please tell us what you saw?"

"I've been trying to remember everything. When that woman and Kit came in we gave them the front table by the stage because Kit was on crutches. I showed them to the table myself and made sure Kit was okay. This place was crowded, especially for a Monday night. But when it's hot people don't like to stay home. We finally got everyone seated, and then . . . Georgina?"

"Yes, that's her name," Regan answered.

"Georgina came hurrying past me, heading for the front door. I wanted to tell her that the show was about to start and she should go back to her seat but there was something strange and intimidating about her—"

"You got that right," Kit said. "Something strange."

"I saw her quickly light a cigarette as soon as she got outside. I figured she'd take a few puffs and be right back." Becky paused, then frowned. "I watched her take her first puff. It wasn't really a puff. It was a long, hard drag."

"She told me she was trying to quit," Kit said sarcastically.

"Then what happened?" Regan asked.

"Then someone came up to me and asked if they could change their table. They said they couldn't see very well. We were just about full. I came back here with them and moved them to a table that I didn't think was any good, but they liked it better. When I went back to my post I looked out and saw this really tall blond guy asking Georgina for a cigarette."

"Had he been in here?" Regan asked.

Becky shook her head. "I don't think so. The bar was empty by this time, and everyone had been seated. The only one out front was the bartender who was busy filling the waitress's orders for the back tables. Clear as day, I could see Georgina's face all lit up and smiling when she handed him the cigarette. I definitely remember that. You know that look a girl can get when a cute guy pays attention to them?"

"I somehow remember having that look myself," Kit

commented. "It was a long time ago."

"Well, suddenly she seemed like a different person. All smiles. She hit him on the arm, playfully, and they laughed about something."

"She hit me on the arm in the cab," Kit grunted. "I'm pretty sure it's now black and blue."

Becky nodded at Kit, then continued. "Then I had to look at our reservations list and count the number of people we had seated. So my head was down for a few minutes. When I looked up they were getting in a cab."

"What kind of cab?" Regan asked.

"Just a regular four-door sedan. It looked old. He opened the door, she hopped in, and he got in behind her. Then they were off. I have to say I was surprised. I was wondering if Kit, whose name I didn't know then, was sitting all alone."

"Is there anything else you can tell us about the guy Georgina left with?" Regan asked.

Becky folded her hands. "The first thing you notice about him is how tall he is. At least six four. Tall and thin. Blond. He had the kind of haircut most guys seem to have—parted on the side. It curled a little on the ends. I saw his profile. My impression was that he was cute . . . and a few years younger. He had a baby face."

"What was he wearing?" Regan asked.

"Jeans and a short sleeve shirt."

"What color shirt?"

"I'm not sure. It might have been green or blue."

"Is there anything unusual at all you can remember about him or the way they interacted?" Regan asked intently. "Anything at all that might seem insignificant?"

"I'm trying to think . . . oh . . . when she was getting in the cab he looked at his watch. But there was something else. I'm trying to think of what it was. This is so frustrating—I know!"

"What?" Regan, Kit, and Billy asked in unison.

"He was a lefty! His watch was on his right hand. I could tell he was left-handed."

"Well, that could help," Regan said encouragingly. She'd been hoping for more descriptive information but how much could she expect? "If you would, just keep thinking about it. I know the bartender is cleaning up, but could you ask him to join us for a minute."

"Sure," Becky said cheerfully. "As my grandma used to say, two heads are better than one."

10

"Hey, you're a lot of fun."

Georgina smiled at Chip, the young man she'd met outside Larry's Laughs. After leaving the comedy club, they'd been on their way to hear a jazz band down in the East Village when the lights went out. Immediately changing their plans, they got out of the cab at one of the popular bars on Second Avenue in the

Fifties where large glass doors opened out onto side-walk tables. Patrons, most of whom were in their twenties, were standing outside, drinking, enjoying the excitement of the blackout. "You're a lot of fun, too," Georgina replied with a smile. "I love people who are spontaneous."

"This place has a great bar on the roof. Let's go." As they started up the dimly lit stairs, people coming down were squeezing past the ones headed up. No one seemed to mind. Chip grabbed her hand. So far so good, Georgina thought.

Upstairs, the bar was to the left. If there were any tables, they couldn't be seen. It was a giant, noisy cocktail party. "What can I get you to drink?" Chip asked. "If you stand over by the wall, I'll make my way over to the bar."

"Normally I'd love a margarita. But I think with all the confusion a glass of white wine would be fine."

"I'll see what I can do."

While Georgina waited, she observed all the young people around her. Everyone seemed so happy and carefree. I never had the chance to be like that, she thought. I never felt comfortable in these big groups. Why is it so easy for everybody else? The three months she'd been with Huck she'd been happy, but then he'd dumped her for her roommate at college. Georgina spotted a young couple. He was blond. He put his arm around his girlfriend and kissed her. The girl giggled and threw her arms around him. Georgina felt her anger building. That's the way Huck and I once were. You're going to be sorry, Huck, she thought. I'm going to get you. I'm going to find out where you disappeared to and you'll be sorry.

"Where did you go?" Chip asked. "It's like you're a million miles away."

Georgina turned. He was holding two margaritas. That's what Huck would have done for her when they were happy together. "I knew you were a nice guy," Georgina said with a laugh.

They clinked glasses. "Welcome to New York City," he said. "You picked some night to be here."

"I'm glad I picked this night," she said flirtatiously. "I met you, didn't I?"

Chip smiled broadly. "That you did. I've never connected with someone so fast. Wow! You were going to that comedy club by yourself?"

"Yes. I'm here on business, and no one else wanted to join me. I wanted to get out of the hotel and I love comedy clubs."

"We could have stayed there."

Georgina sipped her drink. "Sure. But when you said you liked jazz it just seemed like a better idea to head downtown."

"You're here for work?" he asked, moving closer to her.

"Yes. I buy clothes for a boutique in California. I enjoy it but now I'm ready for a change. I'd like to do something where I really help people." She smiled up at him.

"I know what you mean. I work in finance down on

56

Wall Street but I don't think it's for me. I was going into Larry's tonight because I'm thinking of trying my hand at stand-up comedy."

"Did you make a reservation?"

"Nah. Sometimes I just wander into a comedy club to see what the comedians are doing. I'm getting up the courage to take a class at night. I figure it'll be fun no matter what happens. Except when my father hears about it, of course." Mimicking his dad, Chip said, "I paid for your education and you want to do what?"

Georgina laughed. "That is so great you want to do stand-up!" As they sipped their drinks and chatted, the bar was getting louder and more crowded. Chip bought them each a second margarita. Finally, Georgina looked around and said, "Why don't we take a walk? People are out on the streets. Maybe you'll get some good stories for your future stand-up act. At your first performance, I want a front row seat."

Chip's eyes lit up. "Some girls I talk to about this think I'm crazy. Not you."

"You're not crazy."

"It's great to be with someone supportive," Chip said as he took her hand and led her down the crowded staircase. Outside, they turned left and strolled up Second Avenue.

"Where would you like to go?" Chip asked.

"Let's just walk for a little while. Later I'd like to take a stroll down by the river. With all the lights out I'm sure the skyline of New York will be just breathtaking."

"Anything you want," Chip said, his words slightly

slurred. "My lady Rose, the night is yours."

Georgina smiled. She was glad to see the drinks were hitting him. He hadn't even realized she'd been pouring her drinks into his cup.

"Rose is such a pretty name," Chip continued. "Were you named after anyone in your family?"

"No." Georgina shrugged. "Were you?"

"My dad. But Chip isn't my real name."

And Rose isn't mine, Georgina thought wickedly. We have so much in common.

11

Conrad's conversation with his ex-wife Penny was thoroughly agitating. She knew how to get under his skin, push all his buttons, and needle him with seemingly innocent remarks.

The worst part was, he knew he deserved it. Penny was a very attractive woman, and they'd had a wonderful marriage. A wonderful marriage until Conrad suffered a midlife crisis and fell into the vixen Lorraine's clutches.

"She certainly chose a luxurious new hotel to stay in now that the loft has been sold," Penny said softly. "I hear they charge a fortune for a room. Will she be there until she finds a new place to live?"

"No, she won't," Conrad answered firmly.

"Do you think she'll apartment hunt in Greenwich? There are some lovely—"

"You know she prefers the city," Conrad interrupted.

"Well that's good to hear. You wouldn't want to be bumping into her around town. You do like your own space, don't you?" Penny cleared her throat. "Now, don't forget. We have Alexis's twenty-first birthday party here at the house a week from Saturday."

"I haven't forgotten."

"That's good. I had Rod up here today with his crew. They spruced up the pool house. It needed painting and a few repairs. He really is marvelous."

"Rod's a contractor. I didn't think he did sprucing."

"For the right price he does. It's only a couple days' work. You'll get the bill."

Conrad squirmed. Soon he'd be paying the expenses of two ex-wives. It was galling.

"It was good to see him. It had been a while. You didn't tell me he was doing the renovation on the loft for your old neighbors."

"They told me they were looking for a good contractor. I recommended Rod because he'd done such beautiful work on our house years ago. I probably should have kept my mouth shut. I don't need him discussing my business with you."

"He didn't, dear. He's such a sweet man."

"A sweet man when he shows up. Is he finished?"

"No. He promised me today and tomorrow. They worked until it got dark and then left. They must have been on the road when the blackout struck." Penny yawned. "Okay, darling. Would you like me to record the news in case Lorraine comes on again?"

"That won't be necessary. Good night, Penny." Conrad hung up the phone. He was tempted to pour himself another drink but decided against it. His reflection in the mirror behind the bar was of an attractive, graying man who was in reasonably good shape but whose face showed serious signs of stress. He needed to focus and get to work. With fire in his belly, he sat down at his antique desk. The sight of the red leather desktop, delicate china lamp, and engraved Mont Blanc pen set soothed him. He was ready to tackle what needed to be tackled. As Grandpa Spreckles used to say, "Whenever the world was getting me down, I headed into the kitchen and got to work on a new batch of chocolates. That was when I invented some of our finest recipes."

Conrad looked up at the portrait of Grandma and Grandpa Spreckles that had been painted in honor of their fiftieth wedding anniversary. They'd be mortified to know how much money generated from the sale of Spreckles chocolates had been paid out to Conrad and his brother, Winston's, ex-wives. At least Winston now seemed happy with wife number two.

"I'm not going to let Lorraine take me to the cleaners!" Conrad promised his grandparents. He quickly unlocked the file drawer where he kept his financial statements from the last few years. He knew he didn't pay enough attention to personal money matters. He left it to his accountant, whom he trusted completely. After all, it was the accountant who had urged him to have a prenuptial agreement. Thank God

I made her sign it, he thought. Of course she hadn't been too happy about it. She almost talked him out of it. At least I'd kept my wits about me in that situation. She'll only get five million dollars.

It only took a few moments of perusing the statements for Conrad's face to turn beet red. He knew that Lorraine charged every purchase she possibly could. She'd charge a stick of gum if it were allowed. She claimed that it built up their mileage on the airlines. Mileage they were never able to use when they traveled. Their trips always seemed to take place either during the airlines' blackout dates or when first-class award seats were already long gone.

The credit card bills were approved by Conrad and then sent off to the accountant who paid them. Conrad had also given Lorraine plenty of cash for walking-around money. God knows what she needed it for since everything she bought went on the charge card. But now as he looked through his records he realized that in the past two years she'd withdrawn thousands and thousands of dollars in cash from the three checking accounts. Five hundred here from an ATM machine in New York City. Six hundred there from an ATM machine in Greenwich. Why hadn't the accountant pointed it out to him? Conrad opened his drawer and pulled out his calculator. He furiously began tapping away at the keys. It totalled nearly seventy thousand dollars!

"Where is all that money?" he squealed. "She must have it stashed away somewhere. Or she has a separate bank account I don't know about." He shook his head and continued mumbling. "It's more likely she stashed it. She never planned for this marriage to last."

He got up from his desk and stormed out of the room without a glance at his grandparents' faces. He was too ashamed to look at them. How could he have been so careless?

If she hid that money in this house, I'm going to find it, he thought. I'll go from room to room and tear everything apart. He stopped in his tracks as he approached the grand staircase. Could she have hidden money somewhere in the loft? He had taken pains to make sure it was completely cleared out on moving day. Everything she'd left there was now in the guest room. Her purses, clothes, yoga mat.

No use thinking about the loft now, he decided as he grabbed the polished wood banister and charged up the steps. First things first.

He knew that money had to be somewhere.

And as Grandpa Spreckles used to say, "It's not always about the money, it's about the principle involved."

You've got that right Grandpa, Conrad thought wildly. He strode into the guest room, opened the closet door, and reached for the first in the preposterously long lineup of Lorraine's designer handbags.

12

Before the blackout hit, Rod had been chatting amiably with his two employees as they rode home together from Connecticut in the company van. Frank and Wally had worked for Rod for years. They were both single and in their early thirties. Rod had just turned forty and was the father of two young children. The three of them lived not far from each other in northern New Jersey, where they'd all grown up.

"This job is a piece of cake, isn't it?" Rod asked rhetorically as they tooled down the highway. "And Mrs. Spreckles certainly put out a nice spread at lunchtime. When you think the way some clients don't even offer us a morsel, not even a drop of water . . ."

"She likes to talk," Frank commented, himself a man of few words.

"That she does." Rod laughed. He was always cheerful which was amazing, considering how often he had to listen to people yell at him, sometimes quite heatedly, for not showing up when promised or still not having their homes finished months after the estimated completion date. Rod let it all roll off his back. His eyes never seemed to stop twinkling and his cherubic face was often lit up with a smile. The work he did, when it was finally completed, was always superb. Satisfied clients soon forgot their fury and recommended Rod to their friends.

"I mean really talk," Frank said. "I was afraid she was going to fill us in on everything that has happened in her life since we were there ten years ago. She also asked a lot of questions about her ex-husband's loft."

In the backseat, Wally's stomach did a somersault. Nicknamed for his walrus moustache, he had a hangdog look but was always pleasant company. Now his whole body was tensing up. His friend Arthur was sneaking into the loft tonight to check out the hidden safe Wally had discovered last week. A discovery he never mentioned to his boss.

It was the contractor's ultimate fantasy—to stumble upon a hidden treasure in a home that was under renovation. There were countless stories of cash found in walls, jewels hidden under floorboards, sterling silver covered by loose insulation in the corner of the attic. Treasures that the owner of the home didn't even know about, left behind by previous owners who had died or just plain forgotten about their valuables.

A few years back, Wally had ripped a medicine cabinet out of the wall and was stunned to find a diamond necklace in the hollowed-out space. He'd put it right in his pocket, and it was never missed by anyone. He reasoned that he wasn't stealing because whoever owned the necklace was long gone, one way or another. Those diamonds whetted his appetite for more exciting discoveries. He'd been disappointed over and over again when they started new jobs. It seemed nothing like that would ever happen again.

Until last Friday.

Wally had started moving the heavy boxes of Italian tile into the Reillys' front closet so they'd be out of the way. He opened a cabinet in the closet that was close to the floor, a cabinet which he thought he'd thoroughly inspected when they started the job, and slid one of the boxes to the back with greater force than he intended. A funny sound made him nervous. He was afraid he might have cracked the tile. When he pulled the box back out, a false back fell forward. A safe was staring him in the face, its key sticking out of the lock.

Adrenaline shot through his body. Frank and Rod had gone up to check something on the roof, so he was alone. This discovery was his! Knowing it was probably futile, Wally leaned forward and tried to turn the key. It wouldn't budge. He needed the passcode or the owner of the safe's fingerprint for the key to work. The latter was impossible and figuring out the former was about the same. But he knew someone who might be able to figure out how to open it.

Wally's mind was racing. He reasoned that the Reillys couldn't have known about the safe. If they had, they wouldn't have left the key there. They'd also wanted to build new cabinets in this closet and never once mentioned the hidden safe. Conrad Spreckles couldn't have known about it, either. He'd stripped the apartment clean of anything worth a nickel. If this safe had been his, he would have taken it with him.

Wally was sure that there were treasures lying within it, treasures with his name written all over them. He quickly replaced the cabinet's false back and finished storing the boxes of tile. They were due to leave in a few minutes. Finally, he thought! Finally it's paid off that I duplicated keys behind Rod's back. Ever since he'd found the necklace he'd had keys made for every house or apartment they worked on. He thought he might discover something he couldn't carry out in his pocket. Hopefully he had!

Wally couldn't wait to get home. As soon as Rod dropped him off, he raced inside, called his poker buddy, Arthur, and offered to buy him a drink at the corner bar. Arthur, a computer geek who was a whiz at mathematics and loved every kind of numerical gadget almost as much as he loved a free drink, jumped at the invitation. But when he was served his beverage of choice and heard about Wally's plan for him to go into a loft and try to break the code of a safe, he refused.

"I don't need to take that kind of risk," he stated firmly, his thin face looking pained, his pale eyes astonished. He shook his head back and forth and jutted out his lower lip. "No no no. Ah-ah."

"Arthur, we could pick up some extra money. You could buy another computer or two."

Arthur's eyes blinked several times. Thoughtfully, he took a sip of the frosty beer Wally had paid for. "Why don't you have me up there when you're working alone? Don't you work by yourself some-times?"

"Yes, but that's unlikely to happen on this job. And the woman who owns the loft is home a lot. She and her husband are living there while the work is being done."

"Then aren't they there now?"

"No! They're away for several days. Rod said we don't have to go back to work there until next Wednesday when they'll finally be back."

Unbeknownst to Wally, Regan Reilly had been expecting them on Tuesday.

Arthur adamantly refused, drank his beer, and went home to his computer. On Saturday and Sunday, Wally tried again. Arthur remained stubborn, a mulish expression plastered on his face as he swilled all the beers charged to Wally's growing tab.

Then today, Wally had heard from the first Mrs. Spreckles that the second Mrs. Spreckles was on her way back from England, that she didn't know the loft had been sold, and that she certainly wouldn't be happy about it because she was there all the time. Without her husband.

Wally immediately realized that the safe had to be hers, and that he had to act right away. If she had valuables in there, she'd certainly try to get them back. He had to beat her to it. In the back of his mind, Wally realized that this was more like stealing than just finding something left behind, but he didn't care. He was on a wild ride, and the proverbial train had left the station. Saying he wanted to stretch his legs, Wally casually strolled out to Mrs. Spreckles's expansive back yard and called Arthur yet again. Luckily, Arthur had just lost a load of money at the track. All his fancy calculations figuring out which horses should win, place, and show, taking into account all the variables of the race, failed him miserably. Reluctantly, he agreed to go into the loft after dark and attempt to crack the code of the safe. He told Wally to try to find out the date of Lorraine's birthday. People often used some combination of their day, month, and year of birth as their passcodes on everything from ATM machines to alarm systems. It was a stupid thing to do because it made it easier for thieves to break the codes.

"If I can't crack the code," Arthur said nervously, "I'll break open the safe with a sledgehammer. My grandmother hid her jewelry in her attic for years but the insurance company made her get a safe. Thieves broke in and bashed it open. It looked like a crumpled soda can!"

Wally hung up, went back into the house, and without much prodding, learned from Penny Spreckles that Lorraine Lily was thirty years old, only nine years older than their daughter, which of course was disgraceful. She'd turned thirty on the first of January and still hadn't really made it as an actress, which meant, well, you know.

Wally returned to the yard and called Arthur back with the information, minus the editorial. Now as he rode in the back of the Rod's Renovations van, he was a nervous wreck. If anything happened and they got caught . . .

He was lost in thought when the lights went out on the highway. Rod flipped on the radio, and they heard the news of the blackout. Rod immediately called his wife, who said their power was off but she and the kids were fine. Frank didn't call anybody. Neither did Wally.

A short while later, Wally's cell phone rang. He could see it was Arthur calling, but he was too afraid to answer. He couldn't risk having Rod or Frank overhear the conversation. Was he imagining it, or did the ring itself sound angry?

"Aren't you going to answer your phone?" Rod asked. "Someone might be checking up on you to see if you're okay. Or someone might need you."

"Nobody needs me," Wally joked as he pressed the silence button. "Nobody cares."

Frank rolled his eyes.

"Oh, come on," Rod said with a laugh. "I bet whoever is calling is just dying to get a hold of you."

Truer words have never been spoken. At the other end of the line, Arthur was an enraged, quivering mess. Calling from the safety of his car, parked down by the Hudson River, he wanted to blast Wally for giving him the wrong information about when the owners of the loft were expected back from their vacation. And he was terrified because he'd lost the stun gun he'd just bought on the Internet when he was visiting his grandmother in Nebraska. He'd only bought it for his own protection. He bought one for his grandmother, too. If they find it and trace it back to him . . .

"Answer the phone!" he screamed at Wally's recording. "Answer your stupid phone!!"

13

W hen Kent, the bartender, sat down with Regan, Becky, Kit, and Billy in the back room of Larry's Laughs, he was drying his hands with a small towel, then used it to wipe the sweat from his forehead. Women customers found the red-headed, freckled, thirty-three-year-old cute and friendly. "It's not easy cleaning up this place in the dark," he began. "What a job trying to settle everyone's check with all the lights out. Businesses all over the city are losing money tonight." He paused. "I shouldn't be complaining. The situation you're dealing with is much more serious."

"It looks that way," Regan said. "As you know, this woman Georgina left Kit stranded here tonight. Becky saw her get in a cab with a tall, young guy with blond hair. She also noticed he was left handed. If you could tell us what you saw . . ."

Kent tapped the table with his fingers. "It was crowded when Kit and Georgina first came in but I noticed them because Kit was on crutches. Then about twenty minutes later, I saw Georgina hurry past the bar and go outside. She had an unlit cigarette in her hand, so I knew the drill. She'd run out for a few puffs and be right back. The bar was pretty empty by then because the show was about to start, but I was busy filling the orders for the drinks. I glanced out once and she was holding her cigarette and just staring into

70

space. I thought, oh boy, she'll be a tough customer for the comedians tonight. Sometimes you can just tell who's going to be a laugher, and who isn't. She didn't look like one to me."

"Did you see the guy she left with?" Regan prodded.

"Yes. When I looked again, there he was. He was tall, I'd say about six five or six six, and blond, like Becky said. He seemed pretty clean cut, like a preppy. The two of them were definitely flirting."

"Have you ever seen him before?" Regan asked.

"I don't think so. A tall guy like that I would have remembered."

Regan rubbed her forehead. "He could have been on his way inside, saw Georgina, found her attractive, and asked for a cigarette."

"Of course," Kit said, "Georgina might very well have initiated a conversation. Her victims have all been blond."

Regan turned to Becky. "Did anyone not show up for their reservation tonight?"

"Just one party of three and they didn't call to cancel. How rude."

"So he probably wasn't part of that group. I assume you take walk-ins."

"If we have the room. But lately the shows are usually sold out or close to it. Larry's Laughs is getting great buzz. Larry—the owner—is starting a stand-up comedy class. The first session is filled."

"Kent," Regan said. "You said they were flirting. Could you be specific?"

Kent raised his eyebrows. "I see the mating dance going on at the bar all the time, and it always interests me. When I glanced out the window, he was picking something like a leaf off the top of her head. I thought to myself, here we go. Oh—I did notice that he had on a big school ring—the kind with a colored stone in the middle. I've seen a lot of them, but for some reason this one looked huge."

"A school ring?" Billy said. "Wait a minute. This might be nothing—"

"Try us," Regan said.

"I stopped by here on Saturday afternoon to talk to Larry. The club wasn't open yet. We were sitting up front at the bar, then I went to the back to use the rest room. When I was coming out my cell phone rang. It was my mother calling. If I don't pick up her calls I feel guilty no matter what I'm doing—" He paused. "You can see what drove me to be a comedian—anyway, I answered, had a quick conversation about the state of my health and hers, then hung up. When I rejoined Larry, there was a piece of paper on the counter in front of him. He said somebody had just dropped by to sign up for the class, but Larry told him it was full. Larry has nicknames for everyone. Called this guy 'College Boy' because he had on one of those big school rings. Larry was so happy that his class was full. He told the guy he'd contact him if there were any cancellations and would add his e-mail address to the list of people who were sent the newsletter."

"Was he tall with blond hair?" Kit asked quickly.

"I have no idea. He was wearing a college ring, wasn't he? I think it's worth calling Larry."

"It certainly can't hurt," Regan said.

"I spoke to him a little while ago. He's at his place at the Jersey Shore. Let me get my cell phone with his number," Kent offered.

Three minutes later, Kent had Larry on the line. After briefly explaining the situation, he said, "I'm going to put you on speaker," then placed the phone on the table.

"Hello, Larry," Regan said. "Billy told us he was with you the other day, and you nicknamed someone who had come in to sign up for your class 'College Boy.' "

"Yes, I remember," Larry said.

"What did he look like?" Regan asked.

"He was very tall, I'd say at least six five, and had blond hair—"

A shot of adrenaline went through everyone sitting at the table.

"He was a really nice kid," Larry continued. "Very polite. I thought he seemed too normal to pursue stand-up comedy."

Billy rolled his eyes.

"And you noticed his college ring?"

"Yup. It was one of those big, heavy, chunky ones. Like a World Series ring. Must be uncomfortable to have that thing weighing down your finger."

"Billy said you had his name on a piece of paper. Do

you have that paper?" Regan asked.

"I hate to admit this, but I have no idea where it is. I need to get more organized."

"Did you notice what hand he used to sign the paper?" Regan asked.

"He was a southpaw. A lefty just like me. I always notice that."

Becky gasped.

"He sounds like the guy we're looking for," Regan said. "You don't by any chance remember his name, do you?"

"Yes, I do."

"You do?"

"I do because he has a common last name. I thought to myself, if he ends up joining the Screen Actors Guild, his name might already be taken. That's what happened to me. I had to change mine. But this guy's first name was a little unusual so I thought he might be all right."

"What's his name?" Regan asked, trying not to sound impatient.

"Chip Jones. I have no idea what his e-mail address is though. He wrote that down, too."

"Larry, this is great. You're sure his name was Chip Jones?"

"Yes, I remember thinking of that expression 'He's a chip off the old block.' "

"Can you recall anything else he said?"

"I remarked it was a beautiful day. He agreed and told me he'd walked all the way from the Upper East

Side where he lives. That's all I can tell you. He was in and out pretty fast."

"Thanks, Larry. You've been a big help," Regan said.

"What a nice kid. I hope nothing bad happens to him."

"We're going to do everything we can to find him as quickly as possible. If you think of anything else at all, no matter how insignificant, please call." She gave him her cell phone number. When she hung up, she called information. There was no listing for a Chip Jones in Manhattan. There were several listings under C. Jones on the Upper East Side, and several more that didn't list an address. "The trouble is," Regan said to the group, "his legal name is probably not Chip. That's usually a nickname."

"What do we do now, Regan?" Kit asked.

"Let's head over to your hotel and talk to the people from Georgina's company. See what else we can find out about her. I'd also like to speak to the police in Atlanta who are questioning her friend and get a look at Georgina's room if the hotel security will allow it."

"I'm coming with you," Billy said firmly.

"Good," Regan said. She turned to Kent. "Is there a phone book here we could take with us?"

"Yes, I'll get it for you right away."

"Thanks. You and Becky have both been very helpful."

"I'll keep thinking about this, Regan," Becky promised. "Maybe I'll remember something else."

"I appreciate it." Regan started to get up. "Billy and

Kit, on the way over to the hotel, you two can start calling all the C. Joneses in the book while I call Jack and give him an update."

14

Chip and Georgina were walking up a quiet, darkened section of Park Avenue in the Fifties when his cell phone rang.

Georgina squeezed his fingers. "Don't answer it."

He laughed. "Why not?"

"It will ruin the magic."

"Oh, come on." Chip pulled the phone out of the case attached to his belt and glanced at the caller ID. "It's my roommate, Phil. He's a good guy. This will just take a minute. Hello . . ."

A feeling of frustration and dread came over Georgina as Chip chatted with his friend. This wasn't going to be easy tonight even though Chip had been sent to her as a gift. Usually she lured the guys to her car and then drove off with them. She patted her handbag. The knockout drops were in there. Drops she herself used to get to sleep. The small branding iron was in the zippered compartment. And she had her usual supply of lighters. I'm always prepared, she thought.

"You're where?" Chip asked. "Hey, it sounds great, but I'm with someone. We're just walking around. I'll catch you later."

"So you have a roommate," Georgina remarked casually, as Chip stuck his cell phone back in its holder. "Where do you live?"

"On East Ninetieth Street. There's a new bar not far from my apartment that's really popular. All of our friends go there. We can join them if you want . . ."

"No," Georgina said with a smile. "I'd much rather be alone with you."

"My sentiments exactly," Chip said as his cell phone started to ring again.

"Why don't you turn that off?" Georgina asked, trying to sound playful.

"I will," Chip said as he again glanced at the caller ID. "But this is my mother calling. She probably just wants to see if I'm okay in the blackout." He pressed the answer button. "Hello, Mom. Mom? We have a bad connection. Let me call you back." Chip disconnected and then dialed the number of his parents' summer home in Maine. His mother picked up.

"Chip, honey, are you all right down there?"

"Mom, I'm fine. Did you lose power?"

"No, we didn't."

"Well, don't worry about me. I can't really talk right now. I'll give you a call tomorrow."

"Are you home?"

"No. It's too hot to sit in the apartment. Everybody is out on the streets. It's kind of fun. As long as it doesn't last too long. Say hi to Dad."

"Be careful. I love you."

"Love you too." When he hung up, he switched off

the phone, then turned to Georgina. "No more phone calls. I promise." He leaned down and kissed her cheek. "Now where are we headed?"

Georgina threw her arms around his neck. "I have a great idea. Why don't we see if we can pick up a cold bottle of champagne and then sit on one of those benches outside Central Park on Fifth Avenue? It'd make me feel as if we were in a Woody Allen movie."

"You like Woody Allen?" Chip asked excitedly.

Georgina nodded. "*Annie Hall* is one of my favorite movies of all time."

"I have all his comedy tapes. He's hysterical. He's what got me interested in comedy." Chip started to laugh. "I already have a bunch of jokes I wrote about being so tall."

"I can't wait to hear them." Georgina massaged his neck and said softly, "Sitting with you on a park bench, sipping champagne, listening to your jokes— what more could a girl ask for?"

Chip gave her a quick hug. "I'm so psyched you're a Woody Allen fan. The last girl I went out with did not get his humor at all." He reached up for Georgina's hands, pulled them from around his neck, and hurriedly started walking her down the block. "I doubt there are any liquor stores open now, but let's see if we can find a hotel or restaurant that will sell us a bottle to go."

"Whoopee!" Georgina laughed. "This is going to be so much fun."

15

"So how are we going to do this?" Lorraine asked Clay.

Clay sighed deeply. He stood, walked over to the window with the gravity of a deep thinker pondering world issues, and stared out at the vast darkness that was Central Park. "Lorraine?" he began in a serious tone as he rubbed his chin.

"Yes."

"Do you still have keys to the apartment?"

"Why wouldn't I have keys?" Lorraine asked somewhat impatiently. "Until a couple of hours ago I thought I still lived there. But what good is that going to do us now? They must have changed the locks."

Clay smiled and shook his head. "Lorraine, Lorraine. Sweetie, they might not have changed the locks yet. Most times people don't change the locks until a renovation is complete. These people would have no reason to worry that you or the Candy Man would barge back in, now would they?"

"I suppose not. But once they knocked down the wall between the two lofts, their old loft and everything in it is accessible with our keys."

Clay turned to her and folded his arms. "During renovations people usually make sure all their valuables are locked up. They know that workmen are coming and going all the time. The contractor often has keys.

So why bother changing all the locks until the work is all done? There is always someone who can get in. Changing the locks when the job is finished ensures that no one who worked on the place can gain entry at a later date."

Lorraine jumped up. "You're brilliant, Clay! It's so simple, but it took you to figure it out. We have to get down there as soon as possible."

Clay drank in her praise. It felt good to have someone compliment him these days. It seemed that everyone in his life was on his case about one thing or another. He cleared his throat. "There's only one thing."

"What?"

"Is there a chain on the door?"

"No. Conrad and I had talked about getting one but never got around to it. Those locks are heavy duty so we weren't too worried. I just hope the new owners didn't put one on."

"If they didn't change the locks yet, then I'm sure they wouldn't have bothered with a chain. Those things are usually puny anyway. First thing we'll do is try and gain access with your keys. If worse comes to worst and we get caught trying to get in, you can always say that you didn't believe Conrad. You thought he was bluffing when he said he sold the place."

"I knew that you were the one to call," Lorraine said excitedly, as she fluffed up her hair and stretched out her arms like a peacock. "Yessss! You are brilliant! I'll have those letters back in no time. You'll have cash in the bank. We'll celebrate!" Lorraine ran over and gave Clay a meaningful hug, similar to the ones they shared after performing a great scene together in class. You'd have thought they had just negotiated world peace.

Filled with positive energy, Clay joked, "Not that I want to run into these people of course. Who are they? We definitely want to make sure they're not home."

Lorraine pulled back from him, her body slumping ever so slightly. "What do you mean?"

"What do I mean? Who are these people who own the apartment now?"

"They're just a young couple."

"What do you mean 'just a young couple'? Do they have kids? What do they do? What are their habits?"

"They don't have kids."

"What do they do, Lorraine? You're being evasive and, I might add, not a very good actress."

Lorraine turned, walked back to the bar, poured herself another glass of wine, and forced a few tears to roll down her cheeks.

"Lorraine, what's wrong?" Clay asked as he hurried to her side.

"It doesn't matter anymore. I know you won't want to help me."

"I do want to help you. Let's face it, I need the cash, and the money I'll make from selling the jewelry. With any luck that will carry me until I land a series."

"All right then. But you're not going to like what I tell you."

"Try me."

"He's the head of the NYPD Major Case Squad. She's a private investigator. Regan and Jack Reilly are their names."

Clay blinked. "My mother reads her mother's books."

"That's nice."

"She was even hoping that I'd somehow meet Regan in New York and we'd hit it off."

Lorraine rolled her eyes. "Well, you missed out by a few months. She's taken."

"I know. It's hard to meet a nice girl. I've had the worst luck. All the girls I'm interested in are looking for somebody who's rich. If I were a working actor—"

"So our love lives aren't the best right now," Lorraine interrupted. "What's in that safe will help us both with what's most important to us at this moment—our careers. You'll have the money to take classes and audition without having to stress out about other jobs. I'll set those letters on fire and not have to worry about being banished from Hollywood forever." She sipped her drink. "Then our lives will be on course. I know they will."

Clay nodded solemnly. "You're right. This could be a major turning point for both of us. We need to get into that apartment as soon as possible. My rent is overdue."

"It's the fourteenth of the month."

"Don't remind me." He snapped his fingers. "We've got to get moving. With this blackout, Jack Reilly is probably working. And with any luck Regan isn't home, either. You don't have their phone number by any chance, do you?"

"I do!" Lorraine cried excitedly. "I ran into Regan in the hallway about six months ago. It was before she and Jack were married. I told her I'd been waiting for a package that hadn't been delivered yet and I had to run to an appointment. She offered to accept it for me. We exchanged numbers and promised we'd help each other out with deliveries. I have her number in my cell phone."

"What is it? I'll call and see if they're home."

"What if they have caller ID?"

"My phone number comes up as anonymous. Besides, you need electricity for caller ID."

Lorraine quickly grabbed her cell phone off the coffee table, looked up the Reillys' number, then read it aloud to Clay. As he punched in the number he mumbled, "Hopefully they're out rescuing people from the subway."

They both stood quietly as the connection was made and the Reillys' phone began to ring. Lorraine held her breath as it rang several times. "No machine is picking up because there's no electricity," Clay whispered, then added victoriously, "they must not be home!" After several more rings, he snapped his phone shut. "Put on those high heels of yours, and let's get out of here. It is time for us to seize the day!"

Lorraine almost tripped as she jammed her feet into her shoes. "I am never in my life going to write another letter again," she said excitedly, "not a letter, not a grocery list, nothing! I'm not putting anything in writing ever again. And as for that future ex-husband of mine, he's going to regret he did this to me. I'm going to make sure of that!"

"Let's focus on one thing at a time, Lorraine," Clay warned her. "You remember what Wendall always told us to do when pursuing our dreams."

"No matter what anyone says or does to deter you, ignore them. Just keep sweeping the alley. Get the job done."

"That's right!" Clay answered with a confidence he didn't feel. "We have to forget about everything else until we retrieve what's in that safe. We have to keep sweeping that alley." He straightened his shoulders as Lorraine grabbed her purse. "Let's head to Tribeca."

As they exited the suite, Clay tried to block the image that kept popping up in his mind—the disapproving face of their acting teacher.

"Of course, if you choose the wrong alley to sweep," Wendall would say with a laugh, "that, my friends, can lead to even bigger problems . . ."

Clay knew that they were definitely heading up the wrong alley. But, he reasoned to himself, his rent was two weeks overdue.

16

As soon as Regan, Kit, and Billy got back in Regan's car, Kit called Georgina's boss, who she'd spoken with earlier. But Dexter's cell phone went right to voice mail. She then called her co-worker whom she'd dubbed "Gail the Gossip." Gail reported to her that the whole gang was at the bar of the Gates Hotel, including Dexter.

"I grabbed a table the minute the lights went out," Gail yelled into the phone. "The hotel is serving warm drinks and whatever food might spoil."

"We'll be right over," Kit told her. "We want to talk to Dexter and any other people who worked with Georgina. Ask them to stay until we get there."

"Sure thing!" Gail said with excitement. She then attempted to lower her voice. "Dexter is so bummed out."

"I can imagine," Kit said wryly. When she hung up, she just shook her head. "They're at the bar having warm drinks. This girl Gail is something else."

"As long as she keeps Georgina's co-workers around, I'll be happy," Regan said. "Then if I could just get a look at Georgina's room . . ."

Kit wrinkled her nose. "I think it's on a pretty high floor."

"I'll manage. You can wait in the bar with one of those warm drinks."

"I'll go up with you, Regan," Billy offered. "I'm in prctty good shape."

Kit turned to him. Again he was sitting alone in the back seat. "Aren't you glad you came to my rescue tonight?"

He smiled at her. "As a matter of fact, I am. And if I can do my part in saving one poor guy from being branded by an insane woman, well then I'm happy.

I'm telling you, I've dated some weird chicks in my life but . . ."

"We'll have to talk when this is over," Kit said. "I've met my share of wackos, too—right, Regan?"

Regan raised her eyebrows. "There were one or two who deviated from the norm, Kit." She steered the car out onto the darkened street and turned left, heading toward the Gates Hotel. "Why don't you two start making the phone calls? I have the feeling we're not going to find our Chip Jones that way, but at least we can eliminate the possibility. So many young kids in the city have cell phones these days that they don't bother with a home phone. Especially if they have roommates."

For the next ten minutes, Kit and Billy made the calls. A couple of machines picked up, one woman screamed about being called during the blackout because she had banged into a table trying to locate the phone, and others grunted "Wrong number" and hung up. No one they reached sounded happy-go-lucky.

"So much for that idea," Regan said when the list had been exhausted. "If we only knew what this guy did for a living. If he wanted to take a comedy class—"

"Those comedy classes are full of people from all walks of life," Billy said. "And so many of them don't have the slightest idea how to tell a joke. They know nothing about comic timing." He leaned forward. "I don't mean this poor guy doesn't have talent, but he could have come from anywhere. People don't realize how hard it is to get up there in front of audiences and make them laugh. Especially on a bad night when the room is full of hostile, angry people."

"I bet you right now Georgina is laughing at every little witticism Chip Jones utters," Regan said. "Doing her best to gain his confidence."

"Fake laughter has always been so obvious to me," Billy said. "It's worse than no laughter."

"But you like what you do, right?" Kit asked him.

"I love it! I'm just trying to help with the investigation. All I'm saying is that this guy could be in any line of work. Some people say they take comedy classes to help their self-esteem. Are they crazy? When no one laughs at your jokes, self-esteem becomes an alien concept!"

"Okay," Regan interrupted, trying to redirect the conversation. "Kit, your BlackBerry has those information sites, right?"

"Yes."

"Check and see if there's a Chip Jones in IMDb. It's a site that lists people in show business and their credits. If he's not there, we can rule that out."

There was no listing for a Chip Jones.

"That settles that," Regan said as she found a parking space on the street in front of the Gates Hotel. The lobby was a hot, sweaty, candlelit scene of confusion. Overflowing with stranded travelers who couldn't make it up to their rooms and others who had no way home to the suburbs, it resembled an airport lounge during a snowstorm. People were camped out on the floor. Some were snoozing, others talking, others looked miserable as they quietly fanned themselves.

In the bar, Kit spotted the insurance crowd. They were seated at three tables that had been pushed together in a corner.

Gail waved to Kit. "Come on over," she called. "I hope you're not looking for a drink with ice!" She laughed nervously as did a couple of the others who appeared to have already enjoyed several drinks not caring what their temperature was.

At the table, Kit introduced Billy and Regan to her co-workers.

"And," Gail piped in helpfully, "down at the end are Melanie and Dexter who work with Georgina. It's so terrible what Georgina does to these guys. Is that sick or what?"

Regan nodded, walked over to the end where Melanie and Dexter were seated, and shook their hands. "Perhaps we could speak outside where it's not so noisy," she suggested.

Dexter, a somber-faced man in his forties, with thin, wispy hair, pushed back his chair. "Of course. I'm so glad you're here. This is a black eye for our company. A terrible day for Ilka's Insurance. We're all very upset."

Melanie doesn't look upset at all, Regan thought as she glanced at the youthful fresh-faced girl whose blue eyes were sparkling with excitement.

"Do you need any help?" Gail called as Regan, Kit, Billy, Melanie, and Dexter left the noisy bar.

"We'll let you know," Kit promised.

In the hallway, Regan spoke quickly. "We're going to do all we can to find Georgina tonight before she hurts somebody else. But looking for her, especially during a blackout, is tough. We're pretty sure we have the name of the young man she's with but we don't yet know anything else about him. If there's anything about Georgina that you can think of, please tell me now—even a small detail could be helpful. Dexter, I understand you were the one who received the call this evening about her."

Dexter scrunched up his mouth mournfully. "The police in Atlanta got in touch with the president of our company after Georgina's friend was arrested and she implicated Georgina in these other crimes. Naturally, Mr. Blankbucks was greatly troubled and called me immediately. By the time I reached Kit, as you know, Georgina was already out on the town with another potential victim."

"I gather there isn't too much doubt that Georgina committed the shoplifting crimes with her friend."

"No. She hasn't been convicted of any crimes but they have security tapes that don't leave much question," Dexter said.

"And her friend said that she sedates and brands blond men she meets in bars. Is there any proof that she really committed these other crimes?"

Dexter looked at the floor. "There may be. I just received a call from a detective in Atlanta and was about to call Kit when you came in. He is anxious to speak to you, Regan. Georgina's friend said she'd branded a guy in Miami last month. The Atlanta police got in touch with the Miami police. A guy had come forward and reported the incident but apparently Georgina had already left town. The victim's arm was a mess. The branding she does is very crude. The police are checking out all the cities her friend said she hit. They're afraid that many of the other victims are embarrassed to come forward. The victim in Miami had the brand I AM A SNAKE on his arm and gave an accurate description of Georgina. Of course, she hadn't told him her real name."

"Why did this guy come forward?" Regan asked.

"His wife made him. He was married."

"Oh, boy," Billy said.

"What do you know?" Kit harrumphed.

"So it sounds like her friend is telling the truth," Regan said.

"Yes, ma'am. She's looking for leniency in the shoplifting crimes."

"Is there anything else you can tell us about Georgina?" Regan asked. "Melanie, did you know her very well?"

Melanie clasped her hands. "Not really. She hadn't been working with us very long."

"Did she ever talk about her family?"

Deep in thought, Melanie curled her lip. "Just once. I was in the break room at the office putting a cake I'd made for my grandma's birthday in the refrigerator. I was going to her house straight after work. Georgina came in for a cup of coffee and asked me about the cake. When I told her what it was, she looked kind of sad. Usually she had a tough expression, if you know what I mean. She said her grandmother was the only one she was close to in her family, but she'd died when Georgina was twelve. Georgina's father had died when she was a baby, and her mother was always chasing around after different guys."

Regan nodded. "Did she say anything about brothers and sisters?"

"She said she was an only child."

"Do you know how old Georgina is?"

"Twenty-seven," Dexter answered.

"What was your impression of her?" Regan asked him.

He shrugged. "I have to say I'm shocked. I would never have suspected this of her."

"Okay. Can I get the number of that detective in Atlanta?"

"Sure." He reached in his pocket, pulled out a slip of paper, and handed it to Regan.

"Thanks. If there's anything else that either of you think of that might be helpful, please call me." Regan gave them her number. "One more thing," she said. "Kit knows what Georgina looks like. But Billy and I don't. By any chance do you have a picture of her?"

"Yes!" Melanie cried. "I took one with my cell phone during the cocktail party earlier." She slid her shoulder bag off her arm and scrambled to get out her phone. Flipping it open, she quickly pulled up the photos she'd taken only hours before. "Here she is!"

Billy and Regan peered at the picture. The offbeat yet attractive Georgina was standing next to Dexter with a big smile on her face.

"Here's another!" Melanie cried.

It was a closeup of Georgina. There's definitely something weird going on behind those eyes, Regan thought. "Melanie, thank you. That's a big help."

"Can I come with you to look for her?" Melanie asked imploringly.

"I'm afraid not," Dexter said quickly. "Your safety is my responsibility. The boss wouldn't be too happy if something happened to you."

"I'll tell you what you can do," Regan said to Melanie. "I'm going to see if hotel security will let me take a quick look at her room. You can come with me and see if anything up there triggers your memory. Then if you would be willing to sit in the lobby of this hotel and let me know if Georgina comes back, that would be great."

Melanie looked askance. "But then it would be too late! She wouldn't bring the guy back here. Especially if she dumped all the others on the side of the road. She'd get caught."

"You have a point, Melanie. But if she left this guy unconscious somewhere in New York City there's always the danger something more serious will happen to him. And the blackout complicates things. We want to catch up with her as soon as possible, no matter what."

"Okay, Regan," Melanie said. "I'll sit in the lobby all night if I have to."

"I'll join you," Dexter said.

"Great," Regan answered. "Now let's find hotel security. Do you happen to know what floor Georgina's room is on?"

"The forty-second!" Melanie chirped. "Wouldn't you know she managed to snag the best room of all of us?"

17

By the time Rod dropped off Wally at his house in Edgewater, New Jersey, a couple of miles south of the George Washington Bridge, Wally was a wreck. The always cranky Frank had insisted on being dropped off first. Already plagued with guilt, Wally didn't argue. His cell phone was on silent mode but he could see that Arthur had called him twenty-two times. He's not calling with good news, Wally thought. Only people with bad news and stalkers call this often.

Rod's parting words as Wally jumped out of the van left no doubt in Wally's mind about the tone of Arthur's messages.

"Wally, I'll pick you up tomorrow morning to go back to Mrs. Spreckles's house. Good thing she has a generator." Rod laughed. "Good thing for the blackout. Regan Reilly was expecting us in the morning, and I was going to have to make up some excuse. Pray the blackout lasts till at least noontime tomorrow."

"We were supposed to go back to the Reillys' tomorrow?" Wally asked in a faint voice. "I thought we weren't due back until Wednesday when they were home from vacation."

"No big deal. She'll get over it. The job with Mrs. Spreckles was too good to resist." Rod tooted the horn and drove off.

Wally stood in his darkened driveway on his darkened street unable to move a muscle. His head was spinning. He forced himself to walk over to his front stoop and sit. He could hear the sounds of neighbors down the street laughing and talking. He could smell food cooking on an outdoor grill. It all felt surreal. He knew he had to check those messages. Steeling himself, he pulled out his cell phone. There was one screaming message after another from mild-mannered, placid Arthur. *At least I was smart enough not to listen to these in Rod's car,* Wally congratulated himself.

"She walked in when I was there! I locked her out on the roof! Why did you get me involved in your contractor's fantasy? Why? . . ."

As Wally was deleting the thirteenth message, a familiar car came roaring down the block. *Uh-oh,* Wally thought, as he jumped up and fumbled for the keys to his house.

Arthur's car turned and came to a screeching halt in Wally's driveway. He jumped out and came running toward him. *"You idiot!"*

"Come inside," Wally urged in a shaky voice. "We

don't want to attract the attention of the neighbors—"

"I don't care about the neighbors!"

"You should! Some of them are very nosy!" Wally turned, unlocked the door, and scrambled into his darkened living room. "I can't see a thing! I'll get a flashlight or a candle."

Panting, Arthur collapsed onto the couch. "I dropped my stun gun. It was either on the street or in their apartment. I'm pretty sure it was their apartment."

"Stun gun?" Wally called from the kitchen. "What were you doing with a stun gun?"

"You know I like gadgets. They're good for protection. I was buying one for my grandmother so I bought one for myself."

"They're illegal around here."

"I know!"

Wally came back into the living room carrying a lit birthday candle. "Let's make a plan," he said as the wax dripped onto his fingers. "I can always say the stun gun was mine and I dropped it when I was working there."

"That is ridiculous. The owners know someone broke into their apartment."

"You're right. It is ridiculous. I feel so bad for Rod."

"You feel bad for Rod? What about me?"

"He's worked so hard all these years. If this comes out it'll be terrible for his business."

"He won't end up in jail, now will he?" Arthur growled. He wiped his forehead. "I'm sweating to death."

"Okay, okay," Wally said. "I've got an idea. Let's take a ride back into the city—"

"I'm too upset to drive!"

"We'll take my car, then. I suggest we retrace your steps between the building and where you parked your car. It's very possible we'll find the stun gun."

"And if we don't? We're in a blackout! The streets are so dark it's hard to see anything!"

"I don't know. But I have the feeling that at least if we're near the loft, we'll figure things out. Maybe we can grab a bite somewhere."

"Grab a bite? Are you crazy?"

"I can't sit here, Arthur! My stomach is in knots. Let's go. This candle is burning my fingers."

"That woman might still be out on the roof," Arthur said miserably.

"No way. She and her husband are as thick as thieves."

"Thick as thieves? Like us?"

"You know what I meant. He has to have rescued her by now." Wally blew out the remains of the candle and jumped up. "Come on, Arthur. Sitting here isn't going to get that stun gun back."

"I have the feeling that it's too late anyway."

"Never mind. Let's go. But, Arthur—"

"Yes."

"There's no harm in getting the tools out of your car. You never know. We might get a second chance at that safe."

"No way, you jerk! I am not bringing my tools!"

18

Conrad Spreckles searched the guest room high and low. There was no sign of any cash that Lorraine might have squirreled away. But he was wildly irritated, when, upon close examination, he noticed the exorbitant price tags still attached to many of Lorraine's handbags.

"I was so used," he gasped. "Grandma Spreckles would be mortified at this waste! Lorraine bought just for the sake of buying. It's disgusting. She is not getting these handbags back! I'm giving them all to Alexis. Any bag she doesn't like I'll donate to charity!"

In the master bedroom he rifled through Lorraine's dresser. No cash there, either. Just expensive lingerie and scarfs and sweaters, half of them never worn.

Conrad sat down on the king-size bed, feeling defeated. This house has so many places she could have hidden money I could search forever and still not find it, he thought. She probably has a secret bank account where my money is gaining interest. And now she's staying at the Treetops Hotel in New York City which I'll have to pay for. This bleeding has got to stop! I'll call my lawyer tomorrow and see if I can cancel her credit card. I have to limit her spending now or I'll be broke by the time the divorce is final.

He picked up the remote control and flicked on the television. "I'm a glutton for punishment," he said aloud. "With my luck she'll be on the news again."

The phone jangled on the night table. Conrad jumped. He glanced and saw it was his daughter, Alexis, calling. Tears stung his eyes. She'd been so upset and distant since he'd married Lorraine that she rarely called. He grabbed the receiver. "Alexis?"

"Hi, Daddy."

"Hi, sweetheart. How are you?"

"I'm okay. I'm in New York City."

"In the middle of the blackout? Your mother didn't tell me that."

"I'm with Dodie and some of my friends. I was supposed to sleep at Dodie's parents' house down here tonight but I don't feel well."

"What's wrong, honey?"

"This heat is so gross. It's like I can't breathe or something. We're out and have been having fun, but all of a sudden I feel really bad. I'd love to come up to your place tonight. I know you have the generator and I can sleep with air-conditioning, which I know would make me feel better."

Conrad rolled his eyes. She's calling because she wants something, he thought. But it's better than not hearing from her. And until now she had always refused to sleep at this house.

"I'd never ask if I didn't know you'd given Lorraine the boot and she was staying at the Treetops Hotel here in the City."

"I gather you spoke with your mother," Conrad said wryly.

"Yes. She suggested I call and see if there was any possible way you could come and pick me up. I really don't feel well, and Dodie's family's apartment is going to be so hot and horrible. I feel short of breath."

My little baby, Conrad thought. He knew she was just fine but was a creature of comfort who didn't want to spend even one uncomfortable night sweating. Grandma Spreckles would spin in her grave with all the hours she'd spent over a hot stove stirring pots filled with chocolate. Too bad, Grandma, Conrad thought. "Where are you, darling? Of course I'll come get you."

"Thank you, Daddy! I'm at Lonnie's, a bar on the Upper East Side."

"You're not twenty-one yet."

"I will be in twelve days."

"Never mind. Where is it?"

"On Eighty-eighth Street and Second Avenue, right across the street from Elaine's. I know you ate there a lot with Lorraine. Don't come in or anything. Just call when you get close. Take your time, Daddy. I don't want you to rush or anything."

"Of course, dear. I hope you don't get any sicker before I get there."

"I won't. Love you! Bye!"

Conrad hung up the phone. I'm getting my daughter back, he thought happily. But that doesn't stop me from wanting to get my revenge with Lorraine. He stood for a moment thinking about what he could do to make her life miserable. "Ahhh," he finally grumbled, then headed for his closet. "I'll brainstorm in the car." He laughed heartily. If there was anyone on earth who could think up ways to make Lorraine's life utterly miserable, it was Alexis.

19

Emergency workers all over New York City were rescuing people from elevators, firefighters were battling fires started by overturned candles, police were patrolling the streets to maintain order, and Georgina and Chip were on the hunt for a bottle of champagne to share on a park bench.

They couldn't find one anywhere.

They'd gone to Lexington Avenue and walked north several blocks, then south on Third. The liquor stores they passed were all closed, their gates pulled down and locked. One owner was sitting in the front of his store with several of his friends, guarding against looters. He was friendly but was not about to open up for them.

The bars they tried wouldn't sell them liquor to go.

"What does it take to get a bottle of champagne in this town?" Georgina joked as they stood on the corner of Third Avenue and Fiftieth Street. Her anxiety was starting to build. Cute and boyish, Chip reminded her so much of Huck. He must be four or five years younger than me, Georgina thought. He's being nice to me tonight, but he'd never be interested in pursuing a relationship. Her anxiety heightened, and she started to feel angry. He'd end up dumping me just like Huck did.

Chip put his arm around her shoulder. "I feel like we're on a scavenger hunt." He kissed the top of her head. "Your hair smells good."

"Thanks."

He reached down and started to push her bangs to the side.

"Don't do that," Georgina said quickly.

"Sorry. Why not?"

"I look better with bangs, that's all."

He started to laugh. "Rose, there are no lights out here. I can barely see your face." He kept on laughing.

Georgina tried to laugh along with him, just like she did when Huck teased her. Huck, whom she met the first week of college and became the first person she'd felt close to since her grandmother died. They were always together that fall semester. She was so happy. Finally she felt loved again. And she loved him with all her heart. At a raucous party one night at Huck's fraternity, a brother brought out a flaming hot wire in the shape of a Greek letter. "Initiation time for our new members," he'd cried. "If you are truly committed to our brotherhood, you should proudly wear our symbol on your body for the rest of your lives. It's a badge of honor!"

Huck, who'd been drinking heavily, was about to succumb to peer pressure, and allow himself to be branded. Fiercely protective, Georgina managed to whisk him away. The next day he told her he would be eternally grateful. The branding caused a major uproar at the school, and one of Huck's branded fraternity brothers developed a serious infection.

Three weeks later, the day they were leaving for Christmas break, Huck did the unthinkable. He dumped her. Even worse, he did it over the phone.

"I need some space," he told her. "I don't want to be in a relationship right now."

Georgina's roommate, who claimed she was switching rooms after the break so she could live with a girlfriend who had the same major and they could study together, had tried to comfort a weeping Georgina as they both were packing their bags.

"He's not worth it," she insisted. "You'll meet somebody else. You're so pretty and so much fun."

In a daze, Georgina took a campus cab to the bus terminal downtown. When her bus came, she couldn't bring herself to board with the other happy passengers who were carrying gifts and chatting about their plans for the holidays. She just sat there for two hours, staring into space. She didn't want to go home and have to face her mother. Finally she picked up her suitcase and hailed a cab back to her dorm. She'd decided to stay one more night.

When she opened the door to her room, Huck was lying on the bed, cuddling with her roommate. The memory filled Georgina with rage. For weeks, they'd been seeing each other behind Georgina's back. Georgina dropped out of school, never to attend another college.

". . . I mean," Chip continued, "we're in a blackout!"

Georgina pulled herself back to the present.

"I'm going to have to think up some blackout jokes," he said. "Honey, do these shoes match my outfit? . . . What? Who's going to notice?"

Chip was making fun of her.

He tapped her nose with his index finger. "Rose, you are a character."

"Is that what you think I am?"

"I do." He looked around. "Since we're not having much luck with the champagne, why don't we walk over to Fifth Avenue and find that park bench? We've already had a couple margaritas. We don't need another drink, now do we?"

Of course we do, Georgina thought. How else am I going to drug you, you idiot. She knew the knockout drops usually took effect within thirty minutes. Leaning her head against his chest, she purred, "I think it would be fun to have just one more margarita. Then we can take that walk. Okay?"

"I told you, it's your night. I know a couple of bars on the Upper East Side that make great margaritas. We can see who's still serving." He took her hand and they started heading uptown. "One of them is on Eighty-sixth Street."

He's doing this on purpose, Georgina thought. He should know that area of town is going to make me sad.

When he wakes up tomorrow he is going to be so sorry.

So very sorry.

20

Jack Reilly and Keith Waters were standing in the front room of Zora's Menagerie, the brand new SoHo gallery that had been burglarized. Zora's was scheduled to have its opening reception the following Saturday, but the first show was up and had already created a buzz. Specializing in delicate quirky glass sculptures made by award-winning artists from all over the world, the magnificent glass slipper on display in the front window had caught the eye and imagination of many passersby. Now, like Cinderella, the slipper had disappeared into the night, along with more than twenty other glass sculptures. The remains of two of the works of art now covered the floor, smashed to smithereens. Only a handful of sculptures were left untouched.

One of the owners of the gallery, Leon Peters, a man in his sixties with wet, white hair and flushed cheeks was having a meltdown. He couldn't stop waving his arms as he ranted about the break-in and the gorgeous exhibit that had been destroyed. Having run straight from the pool in his apartment building several blocks away with his wife, Zora, he was wearing a Hawaiian bathing suit, matching shirt, and sandals.

"Our treasures!" he cried. "Zora and I opened this gallery to realize our dream. We both love the play *The Glass Menagerie*—we saw it on our first date thirty-five years ago. We both love glass sculptures. After I retired, it finally dawned on us that we should share our love of glass with others. We felt it was our destiny to bring people together in a gallery that was spiritual and aesthetic. People who are sensitive to glass! We worked years to make this happen!"

"I'm so sorry," Jack said.

"Did you know that the Bible stated that glass was more precious than gold?" Leon asked, still motioning wildly.

"No," Jack answered sympathetically. But I guess the thieves must know, he thought.

"I feel as if a piece of my soul is gone. Zora's too! Some thug is probably damaging those sculptures as we speak. Some no good thug who never heard of bubble wrap! Those pieces have to be treated delicately. Every single one of them is worth tens of thousands of dollars. We traveled the world over to collect them. Each piece had its own wonderful story!"

"I assure you, we'll do everything we can to apprehend whoever did this, Mr. Peters," Jack said, trying to calm the distraught man.

"Why couldn't the thieves have stuck to sneaker stores? I hear that's where the big break-ins were during the last blackout." Peters turned at the sound of his wife's voice. She'd been in the back office. "Zora, darling, come here. Be careful of the broken glass."

Zora, a plain, petite woman with a dark tan, was about the same age as her husband. It was obvious that she too had hurried out of a swimming pool. Her wet black hair was pulled back in a ponytail and bobby-pinned to the back of her head, and she was wearing a muumuu in the same tropical print as her husband's trunks. "If I got my hands on whoever did this, I'd wring their necks," she pronounced. "The world is full of selfish people. Selfish people who don't know right from wrong."

"I'm afraid you're right," Jack said quietly.

"We had so many plans," she continued. "Glass is what you're supposed to give as a present for fifteenth wedding anniversaries. Once a month, Leon and I were going to host a party for couples who were marking such a happy occasion." She shook her head. "I suppose that's going to have to wait until their sixteenth anniversary, now isn't it?"

"Not if we can apprehend whoever did this," Jack answered. "We have a great team of detectives—"

"All we know is that they broke through the back-door and the alarm system was out because of this blackout!" Leon cried. "They didn't leave any clues! I'd like to sue the power company!"

Calmly Jack said, "Why don't you two go home and get some rest? I'll have one of my men stand guard here until tomorrow when we can get the door replaced and when we hopefully have the power back on."

"I'm not abandoning ship!" Leon cried.

"But, dear, we're both wearing wet bathing suits," Zora said practically.

"It's boiling hot in here! They'll keep us cool."

"I suppose you're right."

A few moments later, Jack and Keith left the gallery and got into Jack's car. They both sighed.

"This has been some night," Jack said.

"It sure has."

"You don't know the half of it."

"What?" Keith asked anxiously.

"You know Regan called twice about the crazy woman Kit was with," he said, reaching into his glove compartment. He pulled out the plastic bag with the small stun gun. "Before we got home tonight, someone broke into our loft. Regan walked in on them but didn't realize it until she went up on the roof when the blackout struck and they locked her out. They made their escape but accidentally left this behind." He handed the bag to Keith. "I want to bring it to the office and get it traced."

"Someone broke into your apartment? Are you kidding me?" Keith said as he stared at the weapon.

"I wish I were. Now Regan is out on the hunt with Kit for a wacky woman who brands the men she picks up in bars. And a Chip Jones is somewhere in this city, not knowing how badly his evening is going to end." Jack started the car.

"Do you want to send detectives over to your apartment now to investigate the break-in?" Keith asked.

Jack shook his head. "That can wait. There's too much else going on right now. Sometimes these wackos go over the edge. I'd like to help Regan locate this poor guy before he ends up in a dark alley."

21

Lorraine and Clay were passing through the lobby of the Treetops Hotel when the hotel greeter, a man in his fifties with a smooth face and a blank expression, clad in an outfit that resembled that of a Buckingham Palace guard, stopped them.

"Miss Lily," he said solicitously. "Are you enjoying your stay here at the Treetops?"

Lorraine flashed her Hollywood smile. "It's marvelous. Couldn't be better."

The greeter nodded. "I'm so pleased. May I be of assistance to you in any way?"

"Could you get us a cab?"

He smiled. "Why on earth would you want to leave your home away from home, especially during the blackout? Why not stay here and enjoy a meal in our air-conditioned lounge? Our piano player just got here. He is taking requests."

Lorraine wanted to scream but kept smiling. "We're both actors. We want to feel the pulse of the city on a night like this. With any luck, one of these days we'll be in a movie about a blackout. If we don't go out now, what experience would we have to draw on?" She tilted her head flirtatiously.

Bowing slightly, the greeter replied, "Of course. And I do hope that, should you play such a role in the future, you mention that you were able to come back to the Treetops Hotel and relax in luxurious comfort after you completed your research." He sounded as if he were reciting a line from a canned speech.

"I'll make sure the Treetops Hotel is listed in the closing credits," Lorraine laughed. "Now how about that cab?"

"At your service. Your wish is my command."

Lorraine and Clay followed him out onto the sidewalk in front of the hotel. The only lights were from the headlights of the cars that were slowly passing by, none of them cabs. The greeter blew his whistle over and over, ever more frantically, but it was all in vain.

There were no cabs anywhere.

"Can you call us a car service?" Lorraine asked.

"I tried before for someone else. None of them are answering their phones."

"Most luxury hotels have some sort of car that they use to transport guests around town," Lorraine said. "Don't you have one of those?"

The greeter looked personally wounded. "We weren't expecting to open tonight. We have a limited staff," he said defensively. "The employees of the Treetops Hotel are doing their best to ensure your comfort under these conditions."

Lorraine reached in her purse and pulled out a ten dollar bill. "I know you are. We'll walk. Don't worry."

The hurt look vanished as the greeter stuffed the bill in his pocket. "We look forward to welcoming you back to your home away from home."

Not as much as I look forward to getting back, Lorraine thought. "Clay, let's walk over to Fifth Avenue and see if we have any luck."

"Your wish is my command," Clay muttered as they started along Central Park South. The street was dark and fairly quiet. There weren't many people out. On Fifth Avenue there wasn't a cab to be had. They might as well have been standing out in a cow pasture.

"Let's start walking," Clay suggested.

Lorraine groaned. Within two blocks, her feet were aching again. She was wearing her five inch heels, the ones she'd put on in her hotel in England. It was hard to believe that that was less than twenty hours ago.

As they walked south, Clay kept his eye on the road, constantly signaling for a cab or any car that might stop and pick them up. It was hopeless and strange. Strange to be on Fifth Avenue in New York City in almost total darkness and realize there was no way to get a ride downtown. Normally there was always a gypsy cab or a car service driver who wanted to make a buck between jobs. But tonight people who usually took the subway, something Lorraine would never even consider, spent their money on cars.

Lorraine kept teetering along. "Let's stop for a minute," she whined. "I'm getting blisters."

"Why are you wearing those shoes?"

"I told you. The airlines lost my luggage."

"Those are hardly traveling shoes."

"I have to look my best, especially when I'm traveling. You never know when you might meet a producer or director in the first class lounges or end up next to one of them on the plane."

"I wouldn't know. My seat is always in the back in the ultra-ultraeconomy section. Usually next to a screaming kid."

Lorraine sighed. "Clay, I can't walk all the way down to Tribeca like this. I just can't."

"Isn't the thought of getting those letters back giving you strength?"

"I'm getting blisters!" Lorraine cried, stopping dead in her tracks and stomping her foot. But she'd stopped on a grate, and the heel of the shoe she stomped slipped between the metal pieces and got stuck. When she tried to pull her shoe out, the heel snapped off.

"Oh, no!" she cried. "These shoes were my favorite!"

"Your favorites are the ones that give you blisters?" Clay asked wryly.

"I guess so!" Lorraine kicked off her shoes, pulled the heel out of the grate, and stood barefoot on the sidewalk. Despite her disappointment, the feeling of her bare feet on the pavement was heavenly. "Mama Mia, that feels so much better. But I can't walk barefoot, Clay. I might step on glass or a nail or something."

"What do you propose we do?"

"I don't know. Why did that stupid airline have to lose my luggage?"

"I wish I could answer that for you, Lorraine."

"Can you carry me?"

"All the way to Tribeca? No way."

"There's a lot of money at stake."

"Not enough to pay for chiropractors for the rest of my life. Listen, Lorraine, I live on Ninth Street. Let me run down there and get my bicycle. I'll come back and get you as fast as possible."

"You can't leave me all by myself." She looked around. "It's dark and deserted."

"What do you want me to do?"

"I'm scared," Lorraine whined. "I could get mugged."

"Then how about if we go back to the hotel? It's only about eight blocks. I think I can carry you that far. Your friend the greeter is dying to welcome you home. You can shoot the breeze with him until I pick you up on my bicycle."

"Won't that look weird?"

"Lorraine!"

"I'm sorry. Okay. Give me a piggyback ride."

He turned his back to her, leaned down, and she jumped on board. Her legs wrapped around him, her arms around his neck, they started back up Fifth Avenue. "I'll walk the last block," she told him. "To be seen like this wouldn't be good for my image."

"Don't worry," he muttered. "I'll gladly drop you when we get close."

22

Regan, Billy, Melanie, and Cal Hopkins, the head of security at the Gates Hotel, made the arduous journey up a dark, hot stairwell to Georgina's room. By the time they reached the forty-second floor, they were all sweating.

"Kit's lucky she had that bunionectomy," Billy commented as he took a long slug of bottled water.

Cal had handed them each a bottle before they started the trek. "I don't need anyone passing out on me," he'd said. They followed him down the long hall. He stopped and trained the flashlight on the door of Georgina's room and unlocked it with a master key. He pushed the door open. Slowly he started inside.

Regan's first impression as she shone her flashlight around was that Georgina was not a neat freak. There were two queen-size beds, one of them covered with a jumble of clothes. A half-full suitcase was open and on the floor. A quick check of the bathroom revealed the basics most women bring on a trip. Cleansing cream, moisturizer, toothbrush, toothpaste, dental floss, hair spray, makeup, etc.

"Nothing looks too unusual," Regan commented. She took a quick look through the clothes on the bed. She found nothing hidden there or anywhere in the suitcase. A couple of stylish but wrinkled dresses were hanging in the closet. They still had the price tags on them. Maybe the fruits of her shoplifting, Regan thought. Three pairs of shoes were on the closet floor. A quick look through a leather portfolio on the desk revealed nothing but papers regarding the insurance convention. "Melanie, you're the only one of us who knew her. Is there anything here that strikes you odd in any way?"

"No," Melanie said with disappointment.

Regan opened the drawers of the dresser. The top two were empty. In the bottom drawer there was a pillow in a red pillowcase. "Does this belong to the hotel?" Regan asked Cal.

"No. A lot of people like to travel with their own pillows. I know my wife does. She wants a flat pillow and can't stand hotel pillows that are big and fluffy or hard as a rock. Trouble is, she sometimes forgets to bring it home. Our guests do the same. You wouldn't believe the stuff people leave behind!" He whistled. "It'd curl your toes."

"I'd like to talk to you sometime," Billy said. "I'm a stand-up comedian and I'm always looking for material."

"Really? Well, stop by one of these days. I'll show you our lost and found department. If you can't find a few jokes from what piles up in there, then you should give up on comedy."

"Thanks," Billy muttered. "I accept your challenge."

Something made Regan pull the pillow out of the drawer. The red pillowcase looked worn out. She walked over to one of the beds and slid the pillow out of its case. The zipper of the stained shabby pillow was partially separated from the pillow itself.

"I wonder why she doesn't get a new one," Melanie commented. "I know she makes good money. I mean, she makes more than I do and my pillow doesn't look like that."

Regan unzipped the rest of the zipper and reached inside. Her fingers touched on what felt like small pieces of thick paper. She reached and pulled them out. "Photographs," she murmured. Quickly Regan placed six photos next to each other on the bed. As she and Cal shone their flashlights over the images, they all gasped.

Five photographs were of different men's arms with angry red welts that spelled out I AM A SNAKE with varying degrees of clarity.

"Her friend wasn't kidding!" Melanie said. "Oh, my God! She is so cruel!" Unconsciously, she rubbed her arms. "Regan, you have to find that guy tonight."

"I intend to do my best. Now what about this?" The sixth picture was of a young girl of about ten, standing in front of a redbrick restaurant with a woman who appeared to be in her sixties. There was a neon sign in the window that was hard to decipher. "I wonder if this is Georgina with her grandmother."

"Who else's picture would she keep in her pillowcase?" Melanie asked as she stared at the photo. "She told me she was so close to her grandmother. The girl looks like it could be Georgina . . ."

Cal took the picture in his hands and studied it. "Wait a minute! I recognize that place and that woman!"

"You do?" Regan asked, astonished.

"It was a little hole-in-the-wall called Nunzio's on the Upper East Side. I used to go there more than twenty years ago with my friends. It was open until four in the morning and was always jammed. This lady was the bartender! She was one tough broad but she made the best margaritas in town!"

"Are you sure?" Regan asked.

"Yes! This woman had a picture of her grand-daughter behind the bar." Cal smiled. "She bossed everybody around. Especially when she saw a guy who wasn't treating a girl right. She threw more people out of that joint." He paused. "She used to say they should be boiled in oil . . . We all got a big kick out of her."

They were all silent for a moment. "She made margaritas?" Regan asked.

"Yes."

"Kit said Georgina drank a margarita tonight. You say the bar isn't there anymore?"

"No. The woman died in a terrible car accident years ago when she was on vacation. The owner eventually sold the place. I was so shocked when I heard she had died. It seemed like she was going to outlive us all."

"So that's what happened to her," Melanie said softly. "Georgina never mentioned how she died."

Regan sighed. "Cal, where on the Upper East Side was the bar?"

"Up in the Eighties off of Second Avenue."

"Could you get me the exact address?"

"I'll find out for you right away."

Regan glanced again at the pictures of the hideously scarred arms. "We've got to find Georgina. If her grandmother worked on the Upper East Side, she might have gone back up there tonight. Let's get going. I'll call the police in Atlanta from the car."

"I'm coming with you," Melanie cried. "I don't care what Dexter says. He was too much of a wimp to come up here with us. If I lose my job, so be it. Those pictures are awful! I want to help you find Georgina before she brands anyone else. Kit knows what she looks like but she's on crutches. I can run in and out of bars and spot her easier than you can from just a picture. Especially since the bars are so dark tonight."

Regan looked at the young girl with affection. She remembered the way she felt when she was Melanie's age and started to work on cases, fueled by a desire for justice. "It's fine with me, Melanie. But I'd hate for you to get fired."

Melanie threw her arms in the air. "If I can't risk my job at this age doing what I think is the right thing, then when can I? Besides, how would it look for my company if after hiring a nutcase like Georgina, they fire me for wanting to help find her?"

"Good point, Melanie. Now let's get going."

23

Wally and Arthur were speeding across the George Washington Bridge in glum silence. Pointing to the darkened Manhattan skyline, Wally marveled, "That's something isn't it?"

"You don't have to point it out to me," Arthur growled. "Are you forgetting I was already there tonight?"

"No. Sorry. It's just weird that the only lights are coming from the cars on the road." He glanced down at his lighted dashboard, and his heart skipped a beat. There was one light there that he hadn't noticed when they got into the car. The warning light on the gas gauge. They were running on empty. The last couple times he'd taken the car on a quick errand, he'd noticed that he needed gas. But both times there had been a line of at least two cars at the local gas station, so he put off filling the tank.

A bead of sweat trickled down the side of his face.

Please God, he thought. Just let us get to Tribeca. I'll leave the car on the street and walk home if I have to. He slowed down to preserve whatever fuel was left.

"What are you doing?" Arthur snapped. "We're not out for a Sunday drive."

"I don't want to get a ticket," Wally mumbled as he took the exit that led them to the West Side Highway. "The last thing we need to do is attract attention." He kept his foot on the accelerator as lightly as he could while still maintaining a steady rate of speed. It couldn't be more than five miles, he told himself as he gripped the steering wheel tightly. Come on, baby. We've been together through thick and thin. Just get me there, and I promise I'll never do this to you again.

As they drove down the West Side Highway, Wally started to feel better about their chances for a successful arrival in Tribeca. South of One Hundredth Street, the car sputtered.

"What's that?" Arthur spat.

"What's what?"

"What's wrong with the car?" Suspicion in his eyes, Arthur leaned over and looked at the gas gauge. "We're out of gas, you idiot! What's wrong with you? We could have taken my car!"

"You were too upset to drive," Wally protested as he steered the sputtering car to the side of the highway, where it went kaput. "I've been meaning to get gas . . ."

"Meaning to get gas! You get behind the wheel during a blackout, and you don't check to see how much gas you have?"

"I was stressed out!" Hoping against hope, Wally turned the key. The engine whined and moaned but refused to turn over.

"Let's go," Arthur said as he started to get out of the car.

"Go? And leave my car here? It'll get towed."

"Well then why don't you call the police and report it? While you're at it, ask them to give us a ride to

Tribeca." Arthur stepped out onto the street and slammed the door.

My contractor's ultimate fantasy was so misguided, Wally thought as he got out, retrieved two flashlights from the backseat, and locked the car. "If it doesn't get towed, it'll get stolen," he mumbled.

"By thieves who just happen to be carrying a can of gas?" Arthur asked sarcastically.

They started walking along a footpath near the river. As strolls go, if one was in the right frame of mind, it was the perfect time for one. The night—dark, quiet, and calm—had a mysterious, ethereal beauty.

"I hope we don't get knifed," Arthur said with his usual pessimism. "This area is deserted. You don't know who we might come across. That's why I bought the stun gun. Do you know they're legal in most states? But not New York or New Jersey. Ohhhh, no. I read online that instead of having Tupperware parties, women all over the country are having taser parties. They're buying them for self defense!"

"What don't you read online? You're a fountain of information."

"I enjoy my time at the computer."

"Well, legal or not, you might have left the stun gun behind at a crime scene. That's our problem. That's why we're here right now."

They continued on in silence for several minutes.

"Look!" Arthur whispered. "There's someone coming this way." In the distance a lone figure was headed toward them. Arthur's knees started to shake.

"Maybe we should cross the highway."

"What kind of a man are you?" Wally asked with disgust. "Just keep walking. There are two of us and one of him."

As the figure drew closer they could tell it was a disheveled man with a beard. He was wearing a backpack and looking down at the ground as he trudged along, mumbling to himself.

"He's demented," Wally muttered.

Moments later, as they were approaching the stranger whose body odor preceded him, Wally felt a sudden urge to be friendly. "Evening," he said.

The man briefly looked up, lost his footing, tripped, and fell to the ground. "Look what you made me do!" he snarled in a surprisingly cultured voice.

"I'm so sorry. Let us help you," Wally said quickly as he reached for the stranger's arm. But the man swung around and threw a punch. Wally reeled backward, blood spurting out of his nose, as the man high-tailed it down the path.

Arthur, even though he wasn't experiencing particularly warm feelings toward Wally this evening, took off after the assailant. He caught up with him, grabbed the straps of his backpack, pulled it off his body, and gave the stranger a good shove. "My friend was trying to be nice to you," Arthur screamed. "We're going to call the police."

Like a shot, the man scurried down toward the river and quickly disappeared.

Stunned, Arthur was left holding the grimy backpack. He wasn't about to chase the vagrant to an even more remote area. Breathing hard, he turned and walked back to Wally, who had sat down on the ground and tilted his head back to stem the flow of blood. His T-shirt was pulled up around his nose.

"Do you have a handkerchief?" Wally asked in a garbled tone.

"No. My mother told me a gentleman should always carry one, but I guess I'm not a gentleman." Arthur sat down on the ground next to Wally. He placed the backpack on the ground next to him. "I can't believe that nut took off without this. He really must have been afraid of me."

"Do you think there's anything inside that bag that I can use to soak up the blood?"

"I somehow doubt there are any clean bandages, but if you want me to take a look . . ." Arthur said hesitantly. If there was anything Arthur hated, it was germs.

"Take a quick look. Then we'll get going, I promise." Wally reached for one of the flashlights on the ground next to him and handed it to Arthur.

Wincing, Arthur opened the buckle of the backpack, pushed over the flap, and saw that a blanket that had been stuffed inside. "A blanket?" Arthur muttered as he started to pull it out. Right away he could tell that something was wrapped in it. He started to unroll the blanket with one hand and shone the flashlight with the other. His eyes widened as he caught sight of the objects in the backpack.

"What does he have in there?" Wally asked, gazing up at the stars.

"Wally!"

"What?"

"I think that man is a thief!"

"That makes three of us."

"I'm not kidding. There are glass sculptures wrapped in this blanket that are worth a fortune. I read about a gallery that's opening in Manhattan and specializing in glass like this."

"I must have missed that. You read it online?"

"Of course." Arthur pulled a second blanket out of the backpack and carefully unrolled it. "Now I'm sure they're from that gallery!" he crowed triumphantly.

"Why?"

He held up a ruby glass slipper. "This sculpture was the centerpiece of their collection! They had a picture of it in the article. Wally, we are in possession of stolen property! What are we going to do? If we hand these sculptures over to the police, and then they trace the stun gun to me, they'll never believe we didn't steal these ourselves!"

24

In the crowded lobby of the Gates Hotel, Kit was sitting in a folding chair that had been provided by a staff member. Her crutches were on the floor beside her. Dexter, who had proclaimed he would watch for

Georgina all night if he had to, had gone back to the bar to drown his sorrows over his company's pending shame. Kit wanted to keep her eye on the front door just in case Georgina returned. In her heart she knew that there was more of a chance that the Queen of England would appear in the flesh.

Georgina won't be back anytime soon, Kit thought. She is somewhere out there in this dark dark night with that poor guy. If I hadn't gone to the comedy club with her, he might not be in this predicament. If Georgina had gone alone, the timing would have been different. But, Kit reasoned, trying to make herself feel better, she might have picked up somebody else. She had certainly done it before when she was out alone. Still, Kit couldn't help but feel that she was somewhat responsible for the fate of Chip Jones.

A memory that sometimes haunted Kit suddenly came to mind. She was about eight or nine years old and playing outside her house with some of the neighborhood kids. One of the boys asked her for a piece of candy. Kit said she'd give him one of her gumballs if he'd race her around the block on their bicycles. In the middle of the race, the boy went head over heels off his bike and knocked out his front teeth.

Kit had been tormented. If only I'd just given him the candy, she often thought. It was an accident with permanent repercussions. I certainly didn't want to hurt him, and to this day it bothers me. How can Georgina go out and deliberately hurt innocent people? It was so hard for her to fathom. And who's to say that she won't get more violent?

"Kit!"

Kit turned her head. Regan, Billy, Melanie, and the security chief reappeared. Red-cheeked and slightly out of breath, they all looked as if they'd just run a marathon. But they seemed to possess a renewed urgency. "Did you find anything?" she asked.

"Pictures of her victims," Regan said quickly. "I'll show you in the car." She turned to Cal. "I can't thank you enough. You have my cell phone number. When you get the address of that bar, let me know."

"I will. And we'll watch for Georgina."

"Kit, where's Dexter?" Melanie asked.

"He went back to the bar. He's pretty upset."

"He should be. He's the one who hired her. Regan, I'll be right out. I don't care what he says but I do want to tell him I'm going with you."

"You're coming with us?" Kit asked.

"Yes. You and I are the only two who have seen Georgina in person. I want to help." Melanie turned and hurried off.

"We'll be out front," Regan said.

At the car, Regan noticed that Kit made a point of getting in the back seat with Billy. "Melanie will be able to see better from the passenger seat in the front," she said to Regan. "I'll sit behind you. We'll keep our eyes peeled and cover both sides of the street."

"Kit, I think you'll need night vision glasses," Billy joked as he lightly touched her shoulder. "There's not much to see. It's pretty dark."

"Whatever," Kit shrugged. "Regan, can I see the pictures?"

Regan turned on the light in the car and handed the photos to Kit. "Oh, my God," Kit exclaimed as she looked at the images of the branded arms. "She is evil."

"I'm afraid so," Regan answered. "You're about to hear more," she said as she dialed Herb McFadden, the detective in Atlanta. While she was telling him about the photos they'd found, Melanie opened the passenger door and got in.

"We also have reason to believe that Georgina's grandmother, whom she was very close to, lived in New York City," Regan said. "This woman was a bartender at a hole-in-the-wall on the Upper East Side. Supposedly she had a tough exterior, but she kept a picture of her granddaughter behind the bar. Did Georgina's friend Paulette mention anything about her?"

"No, but I'll ask. She's keeps talking about a guy who dumped Georgina in college. I guess he was pretty cruel to her. Paulette says it's why Georgina does what she does."

"If everybody who'd been dumped resorted to this kind of revenge, most of the world would be walking around with brands on their bodies," Regan commented.

"Revenge takes all forms," McFadden noted. "Last week a woman here in Atlanta took all fifteen of her cheating husband's designer suits, threw them in a pile in the backyard, and set them on fire. I guess he should consider himself lucky."

"Sounds like it couldn't have happened to a nicer guy," Regan said. "I'm in my car now with one of Georgina's co-workers, my friend who had gone to the comedy club with Georgina tonight, and a comedian from the club. We're going to drive around the city and see if we can possibly locate them. I know it's a long shot. Has Paulette mentioned anything new about Georgina's habits when she pulled off these crimes that might help us?"

"She just mentioned that Georgina would get her victims to drink margaritas."

"Margaritas?" Regan asked.

"Yes."

"Her grandmother's specialty was margaritas. And my friend Kit said Georgina had one at the comedy club tonight."

"That's interesting. And two or three of those drinks have more of an effect than two or three beers. Paulette said Georgina would pretend to drink while the guys were downing the tequila. When she knew they'd be leaving the bar soon, she'd spike their drinks with the knockout drops."

"Let me know if Paulette has anything to say about Georgina's grandmother. Or any other tidbits she shares that might be helpful."

"Will do."

Regan hung up and turned on the car.

"These pictures are dreadful," Kit said quietly.

"They were stuffed in her pillow. I guess they gave her sweet dreams," Regan said as she steered the car out into the traffic. "There are so many bars in this city. I think I'll call Cal and see if he knows of any bars on the Upper East Side that are known for margaritas. At least it's a place to start."

25

Chip Jones's parents were watching coverage of the blackout in their rustic country home in Maine. Sue and Chris Jones were an attractive couple in their late forties. Both were blond and athletic. They'd raised two blond, athletic children—Chip and a daughter who lived in California. Life had been good to them.

"Chip sounded like he was having fun," Sue told her husband as she sat down next to him on the over-stuffed couch in the great room of the house. A large, stone fireplace was at one end of the spacious room and an open-air kitchen at the other. A cool breeze was blowing in through sliding glass doors that over-looked the sea. The vacation home was their summer retreat and where they spent the holidays.

"What a mess though," Chris answered. "It all started because lightning struck a tree that hadn't been trimmed. A branch falls on a power line and starts a whole chain of events that lead to a major blackout." Chris was a good man, if rather anal. His yard was always perfect, and the tools in his garage and basement were arranged with surgical precision. The idea of untended, overgrown trees was anathema to him.

The phone rang. Sue reached for the portable next to the couch. "It's Natalie," Sue said as she glanced at the caller ID. Natalie was their twenty-five-year-old daughter who was working at a television station in San Diego. "Hello, honey."

"Hi, Mom. Are you okay? Do you still have power?"

"We're fine. It's actually a very pleasant night up here."

"That's good. I'm working the late shift. I just got here and, of course, all the news is about the blackout. When I told my boss that Chip had just moved to New York City, he asked if I could reach him so they could interview him over the phone. I tried, but his cell phone is going right into voice mail. Have you talked to him?"

"Yes, I did. He was out on the town and sounded like he was enjoying himself. They may be having problems with cell phone reception."

"He never turns off his cell phone," Natalie said, worry creeping into her voice. "Where was he when you talked to him?"

"He said he was just wandering the streets with someone."

"Who?"

"He didn't say."

"Do you think he might be with Phil?"

"I honestly don't know. Do you want Phil's number? Why don't you give him a call?"

"Okay. That'd be great."

Sue got up and went into the kitchen. She found Phil's number in the directory she kept next to the phone and read it to her daughter.

"Thanks, Mom. How is Chip's job going?"

"I think that he's less than thrilled with it. But he just started. It takes time to get acclimated."

"Right," Natalie said. She knew that Chip wasn't that happy with what he was doing. But he had time to change careers. He was so funny and smart and likeable that Natalie was sure that he could do whatever he wanted. But she'd always been worried that he was a little naïve for his age. "I'll give Phil a call. How's Dad?"

"Doing fine. We're here watching all the news about the blackout."

"Give him my love. If you hear from Chip please ask him to call me right away."

"Okay, dear. And if you talk to him, let us know." Sue replaced the phone in the receiver and rejoined her husband on the couch. "Natalie is such a worrier," she said lightly. "I can tell she's concerned that she can't reach Chip. It's silly isn't it?" she asked her husband, looking for reassurance.

Chris put his arm around her. "Of course it is. Chip's a big boy. He can take care of himself. You didn't talk to him that long ago."

"You're right," Sue said, putting her head on her husband's shoulder. "I'm sure he'll be fine," she said with a conviction she did not feel. "It's just that he sounded like he'd been drinking a little too much."

A picture of a high-rise building in Manhattan came on the screen. "New Yorkers are being urged to check on their neighbors. Especially the elderly. The heat in the apartments can be stifling and become a real danger for people with respiratory problems. As far as crime goes, several arrests have been made for looting and a number of muggings have been reported, but all things considered it's relatively peaceful. However, the streets are dark and many of them are deserted. The mayor is urging everyone to please be careful . . ."

A sudden dread came over Sue. Her intuition told her that Chip was in trouble. She reached for the phone.

"Who are you calling?" Chris asked.

"Chip," she said briskly.

But his phone went straight to voice mail.

"Chip, please call us. No matter what time you get this. It's very important."

"Honey," Chris said, slightly exasperated. "You just spoke with him a few minutes ago. Maybe he met a girl he's having fun with. He's a big boy. Leave him alone."

"I just need to hear his voice," Sue said. "Maybe I'll call Phil . . ."

"Wait a few minutes. If Natalie's station is doing an interview with him, the last thing you need to do is interrupt."

"Okay," Sue said, trying her best to relax. Like any mother, she had always worried about her children. But this was the first time she had an overpowering feeling that something was terribly wrong.

26

"Are you okay?" Chip asked Georgina as they approached Eighty-sixth Street.

"Yes. Why do you ask?"

"I don't know. Your mood seems to have changed."

"My mood?"

"You just got so quiet, that's all."

"I was thinking. This area used to be known as Germantown. Did you know that?"

"Yes, I did."

"Have you ever heard of the *General Slocum* steamship disaster?" Georgina asked.

"What disaster?"

"The *General Slocum* steamship disaster. It happened in the East River in 1904. A steamship full of mostly women and children was headed to a picnic on Long Island when the ship caught fire as it was passing Ninetieth Street. Over a thousand people died. If the captain had handled things better, fewer people would have been killed. He was sent to prison but eventually was pardoned."

"How do you know all this?" Chip asked.

My grandmother told me, Georgina thought. But I can't tell you that. I can't tell you that except for the time I thought I was happy with Huck, the best times of my life were spent with my grandmother in this neighborhood and down by where she lived. She loved history and knew about everything that ever happened in this city. Georgina shrugged. "I heard about it once and I guess it just stuck with me. Don't you think that captain should have been severely punished?" she asked, her voice rising.

Chip stopped and looked at her. "I guess so. What a terrible tragedy."

"I just hate it when people do the wrong thing and after a while it's forgotten and they can go on living their own life like nothing happened. Most people in New York City have never even heard of that disaster."

"You're probably right," Chip agreed. "Hey, how about that margarita? The bar is just a few doors down from here."

He doesn't even care, Georgina thought. He doesn't care about a major disaster and he wouldn't care about what Huck did to me.

As Chip led her down the steps to the entrance of the bar, he was hoping against hope that some of his buddies would be inside. This girl was starting to act like she was from the twilight zone. What happened to the smiling girl who loved Woody Allen films?

The tiny bar was dark and packed. Chip called out over the crowd to the bartender. "Any chance of getting a couple margaritas?"

"I'll do the best I can. We are really low on ice. It's last call."

"Thanks." Chip pulled out his wallet. He was tempted to turn on his cell phone to check messages but decided against it. He was sure Rose would be insulted. She had been so intent on having him turn the phone off. A few moments later the bartender handed him the drinks in plastic cups.

"Thanks, buddy," Chip said, as he paid the tab.

"Thank you. This has been fun for a while but it's crazy in here with no electricity."

"I bet," Chip said with a smile. He turned and handed Georgina her drink.

"If they're closing soon maybe we should order another drink to take on the road," Georgina suggested.

"I don't want to hassle him again. He's really busy. Besides, this better be my last one. I'm really starting to feel it." Chip took a big gulp of his drink. "Why don't we stand outside?"

"Okay. I could use a cigarette. How about you?"

Chip laughed. "I don't smoke."

"You don't?"

"No. But I thought you were cute and wanted to talk to you."

Georgina kissed him on the cheek and squeezed his arm hard.

In front of the bar, they sat down on the curb. Georgina put down her cup, then reached into her purse for a cigarette. As she lit up, she mumbled, "I'm really trying to quit. But I guess I wouldn't have met you if I weren't standing outside the comedy club smoking. So something good has come out of this habit."

"Sure," Chip said, feeling antsy. He wished they were hanging out with his friends. Rose was okay to be with, he decided, but his initial attraction to her was gone. Something had clicked off. She suddenly seemed so complicated and weird. He took another sip of his drink. Within a few minutes, he'd finished his margarita. Georgina's was basically untouched. She poured most of it into his cup.

"What are you doing?"

"You're bigger than I am. If I drink as much as you I'll get sloppy. And we don't want that to happen, do we?" she asked coquettishly. "I'm happy with my cigarette."

"If you insist. It's so hot, these are going down too easily. And I didn't have any dinner. Nonetheless . . ." he said, then drained the plastic cup. "I'm going to run back inside," he said, his voice giddy. "I have . . . I have to use the little boys' room."

Inwardly Georgina panicked. "I'll come with you," she said quickly. "I have to use the little girls' room." She wasn't about to let him out of her sight. "Besides, I'll miss you too much." She put her arms around him, reached up and kissed him on the mouth, all while removing the cell phone from his belt.

Chip pulled away, started to stand, and almost lost his balance. "Sorry. I feel a little woozy. Those drinks were strong."

"You'll be fine." Georgina laughed as she stood up, draping her arm around his waist. "Let's go inside and use the restrooms. Throw some cold water on your face. Then we'll find our park bench." She leaned her head against his chest and rubbed his back. "It'll be so romantic."

"I can't stay out too late. I just started a new job and I have to get to work early tomorrow morning. I have to be rested and on my toes . . ." he said, his speech slurred.

Georgina's anger was building. He was trying to give her the brushoff. "I'm only in New York for a couple of nights," she said sweetly. "Stay out with me just a little while longer. I promise that before you know it you'll be sleeping like a baby . . ."

27

The greeter at the Treetops Hotel was most surprised to see Lorraine Lily return so soon. He bowed, pretending not to notice that she was barefoot. "Have you completed your research for the evening?"

"Actually not. It's a long story." Her shoes were dangling from her right hand. "One of my heels broke. I don't suppose they keep any extra shoes around here. My luggage was lost . . ."

Once again the greeter's face assumed an agonized expression. "I'm so sorry. However, upstairs in your marble bathroom you will find a pair of terry cloth slippers, compliments of the hotel."

"Terrific. Do you suppose the concierge has any glue?"

The greeter pointed to the concierge desk. "Jon is there and will be happy to help."

Jon was a serious young man with bushy eyebrows who looked as if he carried the weight of the world on his slight shoulders. "I'm sure we can try and reattach your heel with glue but I can't make any promises. If you can wait until tomorrow . . ."

"I can't," Lorraine interrupted. "Do what you can. I'll be right back." She hurried up to her suite and went into the softly lit, beige marble bathroom. White slippers were laid out on a white mat next to the ultra-modern scale. A thick, terry cloth robe was hanging from the back of the door. It all looked so peaceful and spalike. Lorraine looked longingly at the large tub. I'd love a soothing soak, she thought, after which I could wrap myself in the robe, then place my poor aching feet in the terry cloth slippers. Slippers that were never intended for tromping around New York City. She put them on.

If things get desperate, which they probably will, I'll have to wear these slippers on the street, Lorraine thought. At least we're in a blackout. And we'll be on Clay's bicycle.

She glanced in the bathroom mirror. Even though she looked a little tired, she was, as usual, pleased with her reflection. Lorraine knew she was a beautiful, sexy woman. She knew she had what it takes to make it as an actress. A pit formed in her stomach. She *had* to get those letters back. Dashing out of the bathroom, she exited the suite and took the elevator back to the lobby.

"I'm afraid the heel is so thin that there isn't much of a surface to place the glue," Jon gravely informed her. "We did what we could. I wouldn't try on the shoe just yet. You should give it time to dry."

"Thank you," Lorraine said. "I'll hope for the best."

"However," the concierge continued, "we did find a pair of shoes in the closet that belong to a woman who is painting all those gorgeous flowers on the walls of our lobby bathrooms. I'm sure she wouldn't mind if you borrowed them. They are not the most stylish but they are your size." Jon pulled the shoes out of a brown bag and held them up.

Lorraine stared in horror at the paint-splattered, cheap brown oxfords. They were made out of what looked like a velour material and had big thick laces. "I don't know what to say," she stammered. "I don't have socks, so I wouldn't want to . . ."

Jon retrieved a pair of nylon Peds from the bag. "I didn't expect you to fall in love with them," he said gravely, "but I don't advise walking around New York City barefoot. And our slippers weren't meant for the outdoors."

"I can't thank you enough," Lorraine said. "I wish that I didn't have to go out again at all. You are so kind."

Jon stared at her. "Our goal at the Treetops Hotel is to go the extra mile for our guests."

"And you do," Lorraine said quickly. "You all do. These shoes are just perfect."

Lorraine took the bag and hurried out the door,

grateful that the greeter was busy with other guests. She'd wait for Clay on one of the benches across the street where she could keep an eye on the front door of the hotel. He'd better get here soon, she thought, as she started to run across the street in her slippers. One of them fell off and was run over before she even reached the other side.

She collapsed onto the bench, and wearily reached into the bag. I guess I have no choice, she thought. Wait till Clay sees these.

Where is he anyway?

28

As Becky and Kent were leaving the comedy club, Becky couldn't stop thinking about the couple she had seen leaving together in the cab. If only I could do something to help, she thought. Regan Reilly had said they couldn't announce that there was a crazy girl out on the streets of Manhattan with a guy named Chip Jones whom she might harm. They had no proof that she'd carried out the crimes her friend claimed she committed. Besides, with the blackout, who would get the word anyway?

But someone must know this Chip Jones.

Kent was married and lived up in Yonkers. "Becky, can I give you a ride? I'm sure it's tough to get a cab."

Over the summer, Becky was living in a friend's older sister's apartment in Greenwich Village, sleeping in the living room on the Bernadette Castro Convertible. The sister traveled a lot for business and was currently out of town. Becky didn't really want to go home to an unfamiliar, dark apartment by herself. "That's nice of you to offer, Kent, especially since you're heading in the other direction. Do you mind if I just make a quick phone call? A friend of mine was going out tonight with a bunch of people. I'd love to meet up with them if they haven't gone home yet."

"Sure. Let's start walking toward my car. It's parked down the street."

Becky pulled out her phone. "My mother always jokes with me that in her day you couldn't catch up with your friends on a night out if you hadn't planned it in advance. Nobody had cell phones."

"On the other hand," Kent said, "there must have been something nice about people not being able to reach you 24/7."

Becky nodded in agreement as she dialed her friend Alexis. They came from completely different backgrounds but had hit it off freshman year of college. Alexis was wealthy, had yet to work a day in her life, and could be a little snobbish. An only child, she'd had to endure her parents' divorce when her father left her mother for a younger woman. Becky was a scholarship student from a large family who always had some kind of part-time job to pay for her books.

Alexis answered her phone with a youthful urgency in her voice, as though every phone call had the potential to be something wonderful or exciting. "Becky, hi!

Can you believe this blackout?" she yelled. There was lots of background noise.

"Hi! I was working, and they closed the club. Where are you?"

"We're at that bar on the corner of Eighty-eighth and Second that we were at last week. I called my dad to come pick me up, but he probably won't be here for at least an hour. Come on over!"

"You called your dad?" Becky asked, astonishment in her voice.

"Yes. He wants to get back in my good graces, so I knew he'd come get me. He has a generator at his house which means air-conditioning! Yes!"

"Lucky you!"

"Get over here now! There are so many cute guys. You can come with me to my dad's house if you want. It'll probably be a little weird for me to be alone with him after all this time. It's still awkward for us."

"Are you sure it'd be okay?"

"Totally."

"Thanks. Maybe I will. It'd be creepy going back to that apartment by myself in the dark. I just have to get back for work tomorrow night if the blackout is over. You won't believe what happened at the club tonight."

"What?"

"I'll tell you when I get there."

"Cool. See you soon." Alexis hung up, then turned to her friend Dodie whose eyes were glued to the front door of the bar.

"Oh good!" Dodie cried. "That cute guy, Phil, I had

141

just started talking to is coming back inside. When he took that phone call from the reporter, I thought we might not see him again."

"He is cute," Alexis agreed. "I wonder if he has any cute friends . . ."

29

When Jack and Keith got back to the office, there were no leads on Chip Jones. Jack gave the stun gun to one of his detectives, then sat down at his desk and called Regan. "We have nothing yet on your guy. How's it going?"

"We're on our way to bars on the Upper East Side." She filled him in on the pictures they had found and her talk with the detective from Atlanta.

"Our patrol cars are on the lookout for them, especially in isolated areas. Keep me posted, Regan. Be careful."

"I will."

When Regan hung up, she double-parked the car in front of a Mexican restaurant on Seventy-fifth Street that Cal said had great margaritas. "Melanie and I will run in and take a look," Regan told Kit and Billy.

"We'll keep an eye out from here," Kit said.

"It's getting late. A lot of these places have already closed. We have to work fast," Regan said as she and Melanie disappeared inside. The bar was crowded but there was no sign of Georgina.

The bartender looked weary. "There were a lot of blond preppy kids in here tonight. And a lot of girls with highlights in their hair. Sorry I can't be of help."

Back in the car, Regan sighed. "They could be absolutely anywhere. But let's try that other bar on Eighty-sixth Street that Cal suggested." She steered the car up a dark and what felt increasingly dreary Third Avenue.

30

Wally's nose wouldn't stop bleeding. "He got me good. I could use ice and a few wads of cotton."

"This isn't the best night to be looking for ice," Arthur commented. "Do you want me to take you to an emergency room?" he asked halfheartedly.

"For a bloody nose? I don't think so."

The two of them were sitting on the darkened path off the Hudson River just south of Ninety-sixth Street. "We'd better get out of here," Arthur said as he carefully rolled the glass sculptures back in the blankets. "What if that crazy guy comes back with a bunch of his crazy friends?"

"I don't think we have to worry about that," Wally mumbled. "He didn't seem very social. What should we do about the glass slipper and all that other fancy glass?"

"They are considered beautiful and valuable works of art," Arthur said, impatient with Wally's obvious lack of sophistication. "I wish there was a place we could hide them until after we've looked for my stun gun."

"Do we definitely want to hand them over to the police?"

"Of course!" Arthur said indignantly. "It might be the only thing that saves us. Have you ever heard of plea bargaining?"

"Then let's call Jack Reilly."

"Who's Jack Reilly?"

"He owns the loft you went into tonight."

"Why would we call him?" Arthur snapped.

Wally braced himself. "He's head of the NYPD Major Case Squad."

Arthur blinked. "What?"

"You heard me."

"You can't be serious," Arthur spat. "If I had known that, I would never have gone in there, no matter how much money I lost at the track!"

"That's why I didn't tell you."

"I could strangle you, Wally. Just strangle you."

"I'm sure you could. But let's call Jack first. If we don't report the crime immediately, it will really raise suspicion when we finally do. We'll tell Reilly we were coming into town, ran out of gas, and gosh, look what happened. We'll be heroes. At least for a little while. You know, the old fifteen minutes of fame. It certainly won't hurt if they do find your stun gun in his apartment."

Arthur was quiet for a moment. "You think?" he finally asked.

"I think. Besides, if we get up and walk away from here with that backpack, and the cops stop us because they see me dripping with blood, dollars to doughnuts they'll soon realize we're in possession of stolen property."

"I wish I had never met you."

Wally shrugged. "Sorry about that. Get out your cell phone."

"But what about going to his apartment to see if the stun gun is there?"

"That won't work. I'm a bloody mess. If they catch us going into the apartment then handing over the glass sculptures will mean nothing. They'll definitely think we stole them. I'll make some excuse for showing up at the Reillys' apartment tomorrow even if Rod goes to Connecticut. With any luck I'll find the stun gun before they do."

Arthur moaned.

"We can't risk more trouble, and this is our chance to gain points, I'm telling you. Think of how happy whoever owns the gallery will be. They'll probably give us a great reward."

Arthur shook his head vehemently. "Not necessarily! Didn't you read about the woman who dug a painting out of the trash on the sidewalk, recognized its magnificence, then traced the owners who had reported it stolen years before?"

"No."

"They gave her pittance! After all her work. It was pathetic. And how about the contractor who found money in the wall of an old home, happily shared the discovery with the new owner, and then got nothing for his honesty?"

"Do you read any good news on the Internet?"

"The world has a lot of problems," Arthur said sadly. "But I did read about how excited the gallery owners were about all their glass sculptures. They'd collected them from all over the world."

"So let's make their day."

Arthur got out his cell phone. "Do you think information is working?"

"Try."

Thankfully it was. Arthur was connected to the NYPD nonemergency line, then handed the phone to Wally.

A moment later, Jack Reilly picked up the line and identified himself.

"Jack, this is Wally. You know, I work with Rod on your apartment."

In his office, a puzzled look came over Jack's face. "Wally, how are you? Is everything okay?"

"Funny you should ask. My buddy Arthur and I decided to drive into the city tonight—"

As he spoke, Arthur realized what a big mistake they were making. It sounded absurd to drive into the city during a blackout.

"—and my car ran out of gas on the West Side Highway."

"That's too bad," Jack murmured, wondering where this conversation could possibly be headed.

"So we got out and started to walk on the path along the river. A demented guy passes us, and he ends up throwing a punch at me. Blood came gushing out of my nose. It hurts. I bet I'm going to need a nose job."

"Do you want me to send an ambulance?" Jack asked.

"Well, let me finish."

"Okay."

"My buddy, Arthur, runs after the weirdo. That's what friends are for, right? So Arthur pulls off the guy's backpack, and what does my assailant do? Takes off like a scared rabbit. It turns out the backpack is full of glass sculptures."

"Glass sculptures?" Jack asked quickly, gripping the phone.

"Yeah. One of them is a glass slipper. Arthur says he thinks they belong to a gallery that is about to open. He reads everything on the computer."

"There was a theft of glass sculptures at a new gallery tonight," Jack confirmed. "Where exactly are you, Wally? We'll be right there."

When Wally snapped his cell phone shut, Arthur laid back on the grass and rubbed his eyes. "I don't think it was the right move to call the cops."

"Too late now."

Within moments the sirens from at least three patrol cars could be heard racing toward the scene.

"I hope one of those cops has some aspirin," Wally said. "My head is killing me."

31

Georgina parked herself outside the men's room when Chip went inside. The small, dark hallway was not the most pleasant area to wait in, but her anxiety was mounting. She felt as if Chip were slipping from her reach and she couldn't let that happen. He was already feeling the effects of the knockout drops she'd slipped into his drink. She had to take him somewhere isolated and she had to do it now.

The bar was so dark and hot. Disturbing thoughts kept racing through Georgina's head. Her grandmother had worked near here. Georgina missed her so much. Why did she have to die like that?

The bathroom door swung open and Chip stepped out, his hair wet. He was startled to see Georgina standing so close. It was like she was a stalker. "I had to rinse off," he explained. "Let's get out of here."

They made their way out of the darkened bar which was still crowded with people nursing their last drink.

"I really have to get home," Chip said. "I'm not feeling that well."

"What am I supposed to do?" Georgina asked testily. "Walk back to my hotel in the dark by myself?"

"No, of course not. I'll see you back. Maybe we can get together tomorrow night," he added, trying to ease the tension.

You're lying, Georgina thought. "My hotel is on the Upper West Side."

"It is?" Chip said with surprise.

"It is."

"Well, let's start walking. With any luck we'll get a cab."

"I haven't seen many around."

Chip thought about inviting her to stay on the couch at his apartment. It was a long walk to the Upper West Side. But something told him to get rid of her tonight. He could tell she was trouble. He didn't want her to know where he lived. She was moody and strange. A friend of his had a girlfriend like that for a very brief period. What a psycho she was, super nice one minute, a witch the next. His buddy had to change his cell phone number because she kept filling it up with screaming messages. Wait till the guys hear about this one. "Come on," he said.

The two of them started walking up the block. Georgina had the plastic cup with the remains of her drink in hand. She pretended to take a sip. "Here," she said. "Please have the rest."

"That's okay," Chip said. "I've had enough."

"Think of it as the loving cup," Georgina said, her tone commanding. "To finish off our night on the town. I heard it's bad luck if you turn down a drink from a loving cup."

Anything to placate her, Chip thought. There were only a few ounces left. He swallowed the warm liquid and threw the plastic cup in a trash can.

They were walking west toward Fifth Avenue and Central Park. If we have to walk through the park, so be it, Chip thought. No one we meet there could be as strange as this chick.

Back at the bar a guy came out of the men's room and handed the bartender a college ring. "Jay, this was next to the sink," he said. "I almost missed it, it's so dark in there."

"Thanks," Jay answered. "I'm sure whoever lost it will come back tomorrow." He turned to the crowd. "All right everybody, I've got to close up. Let's get going."

After the crowd finally dispersed, Jay walked to the window and pulled down the metal shutters. "A sound I love," he mumbled. "Closing time." He locked up the cash register and placed the college ring in one of the compartments. That's a big ring, he thought. How can somebody forget to put that back on? He must have been feeling no pain.

Jay exited the front door and was securing the lock when a car pulled up. Two young women jumped out.

"Excuse me," one of them said.

"Sorry, we're closed. I've had enough," he joked. "They better get those lights back on soon. It's exhausting working in the dark."

"Please. My name is Regan Reilly, and I'm a private investigator." She pointed to the young woman standing with her. "If we could just talk to you for a minute."

Jay's demeanor changed. "What's the problem?" he asked.

"We're trying to track down a young couple. His name is Chip Jones. He's quite tall, with blond hair. She has long, dark, highlighted hair and bangs. We're afraid she is dangerous and could be a terrible threat to his safety. They might have been drinking margaritas."

Jay blinked. "Gee," he said. "I serve a lot of margaritas. It's what we're known for. I was serving so many drinks in the dark tonight, and the place was so crowded, it was hard to focus on what anyone looked like. But a tall, blond guy did order two margaritas at last call. I didn't see who he was with."

Regan sighed. "I know this might sound crazy but I'll ask anyway. You didn't happen to notice if he was wearing a big college ring did you?"

Jay's eyes almost popped out of his head. "I can't believe you're asking me that."

"Why?" Regan asked quickly.

"Someone left a college ring behind in the men's room. Another kid found it and handed it over just a few minutes ago. It's a big one, that's for sure."

"Where is it?" Regan asked.

"Inside." Without being asked, Jay unlocked the door to the bar. Guided by Regan's flashlight, the three of them hurried into the dark, quiet room that smelled of stale beer. Jay opened the cash register and produced the ring. It was from Chairsworth, a prestigious university in Massachusetts. Regan shone her light on the inside of the ring, then inhaled sharply.

"What, Regan?" Melanie asked.

"It's engraved with the initials CRJ. This has got to

be Chip Jones's ring," Regan said quickly, then looked at the bartender. "Do you know when the tall guy left?"

"It couldn't have been that long ago. Like I said, he ordered the drinks when it was last call."

32

W hen Clay finally reached his building, he walked up the three flights in the dark to his apartment. He unlocked the door, braced himself, and pushed it open. Numerous lit candles illuminated the small living room. His roommate, Bob, and Bob's girlfriend, Diane, were eating dinner at the small table off the kitchenette. The rest of the humble abode consisted of two tiny bedrooms and a bathroom.

"Hey," Clay said. "What's going on?"

"Where have you been?" Bob asked jovially. "Are you hungry?"

"We've got plenty of food here," Diane said almost too cheerfully. "We're eating whatever was in the refrigerator before it goes bad. Can I fix you a plate?"

"No, I'm fine," Clay answered. "I'm going back out in a few minutes. It's too hot in here. A friend of mine is having a party on his rooftop terrace. Maybe I'll sleep under the stars." He went into the bathroom, feeling slightly annoyed. Diane was always at their apartment. She had her own place but shared it with three other girls, so she and Bob spent their time together here. They never gave him a night to himself. Diane was a strikingly attractive dancer with long, curly black hair, and Bob was an all-American-looking actor who was getting a lot of work in commercials.

So let them get their own pad.

Clay couldn't wait to be able to afford to live on his own. Maybe he'd use some of the money he got tonight to find another living situation.

In the bathroom, a pair of Diane's tap shoes were on the floor and her dance clothes were thrown over the side of the tub. Her stuff was always strewn everywhere. Glancing at the shoes, Clay suddenly realized they looked about the same size as the shoes Lorraine had been wearing. Should he borrow them and hope Diane wouldn't notice? He'd bring them back later. Why not? he thought. He went into his bedroom and grabbed a small nylon bag that he used to carry his pictures and résumé and whatever else he needed for schlepping around the city to auditions. Back in the bathroom, he stuffed the shoes inside.

There's no way she'll notice they're missing tonight, he decided. She's such a slob she won't even realize where she left them. Those two are drinking wine and will be asleep soon. Hopefully, I'll be back before they wake up, and I'll be a lot richer. This bag will be stuffed with jewelry and cash.

Clay went back into the tiny living room and walked over to his bike which was parked behind the couch. He started to wheel it toward the door. A funny noise made him look down. One of the tires was completely flat. "What happened here?" he mumbled.

"Oh no," Diane giggled. "I am so sorry."

Clay looked over at her. "Huh?"

"I was running late today, and I had a big audition for a Broadway play. I knew I'd never make it on time with all the traffic, and the subway can take forever. I got so mad at myself, and I knew if I let all the negative energy I was feeling take over my whole being, it would just ruin my audition. So I borrowed your bike. On the way back, I ran over a nail and the tire went flat. I'm really sorry. I was going to get it fixed tomorrow."

Clay stood there in disbelief. "You borrowed my bike?"

"I thought you'd understand. You know how it is when you have a big audition, Clay. The good news is they loved me! My agent is sure they're going to call me back."

I can't take it, Clay thought. I just can't take it. These people are so inconsiderate. He was speechless.

"Hey, buddy, Diane's really sorry," Bob said, trying to smooth things over. "Why don't you sit down and have a glass of wine with us?"

Lorraine is going to freak out, Clay thought. She is just going to freak out.

33

Kent pulled his car up to Lonnie's, the popular new bar at the corner of Eighty-eighth and Second that was a magnet for the twenty-somethings in the neighborhood. Just two weeks old, it had been written up on the Internet as well as in magazines and newspapers. Word of mouth had also brought in the desired clientele.

"Have fun," Kent said to Becky. "But be careful. As we saw tonight, there are a lot of weirdos out there."

"I will. You get home safely!" Becky got out of his car, closed the door, and hurried across the sidewalk. She was thrilled to be able to meet up with Alexis.

Like most places this particular evening in New York City, the bar was hot and dark, lit only by votive candles that weren't exactly resplendent. The floor felt sticky, it was incredibly noisy, but the lively young crowd seemed as if they couldn't be happier. Immediately energized, Becky looked around. Alexis was standing in a crowd at the bar, trying to order a drink. She was so pretty and even though she was wearing casual summer clothes, you could just tell that she was rich, Becky thought as she hurried over. "Hi!"

Alexis turned and gave her a hug. "I'm so glad you're here!" she said excitedly, her brown eyes sparkling, her gold hoop earrings dangling. "A couple of my friends just left, and Dodie is chatting up some guy at the other end of the bar. I walked away to give them some space. Do you want a beer?"

"Sure. I'll be right back, okay?"

"No problem."

It wasn't easy to make out all the faces, but Becky wanted to take a quick look through the joint to see if by any chance the infamous couple who'd left the comedy club tonight were there. She squeezed her way through the crowd back toward the bathrooms, turned around, and came back. There was no sign of them. She passed Dodie, who was engrossed in a conversation and didn't notice her. That guy is cute, Becky thought.

Two beers were on the counter in front of Alexis. "That was fast," she said, handing one over.

"Let me give you some money."

"Don't worry about it."

"Thanks." Becky took a sip of the warm brew. "Alexis, you are so not going to believe what happened tonight." Rapidly, she told the story of Georgina and being questioned by a private investigator.

"Are you serious?" Alexis asked. "I thought Lorraine was bad news. She might have spent loads of my Dad's money but I don't think she ever, like, physically hurt him. I'd tear her hair out if she did."

"I don't blame you! I'd feel the same way if someone tried to hurt my dad."

"You're lucky he's still with your mom," Alexis said, a wistful tone in her voice. She took a quick sip of her beer.

"I know," Becky said, feeling slightly uncomfortable. "Alexis, they think the guy that this girl picked up was interested in taking a comedy class and lives on the Upper East Side. You never heard of a Chip Jones, did you?"

"No," Alexis answered, twirling a strand of her hair. "Most of the guys around here are more into business and stuff."

Becky nodded. "Thanks for inviting me to your dad's tonight. I can't tell you how glad I am not to be alone. You're such a good friend."

"No problem. Now that Lorraine is history, the coast is clear. My dad has a fabulous pool. Tomorrow we can catch some rays. Can you believe that Lorraine checked into the Treetops Hotel tonight? It costs a fortune! Of course my dad sold the loft downtown a couple months ago without telling her. I was so psyched."

Becky laughed. Alexis's and her lives were so different. "Hey, here comes Dodie."

Alexis turned. Dodie was walking toward them, the guy she'd been talking to right behind. He looked distracted.

"Hi, Becky!" Dodie said. "Becky, this is Phil."

"Nice to meet you," he said as he shook her hand. "Sorry I can't join you but I've got to get going . . ."

34

Back in the car, Regan showed Kit and Billy the college ring. "It has the initials CRJ. It must be his. The bartender thinks he was here for last call," Regan said, frustration in her voice. She pulled out her cell phone and called Jack.

"I'll put out the word for patrol cars in that area to be especially vigilant," Jack said. "They're dealing with a lot of problems tonight, but I emphasized this was important." He paused. "And you'll never believe where I'm headed."

Regan listened as he told her of Wally's saga.

"He's waiting for me on a footpath next to the West Side Highway while he nurses a bloody nose. If he really has the gallery's stolen sculptures, I'll be tempted to kiss his nose to make it better. We'll have to give the contractor a bonus no matter how our apartment turns out."

"While they're scouting for the thief along the Hudson River, make sure they keep an eye out for Georgina and Chip. I'm afraid they could be anywhere in this city."

"I know, Regan," Jack said. "I'll join you as soon as I get free."

Regan hung up and put the car into drive. Her cell phone rang before she'd driven ten feet. Quickly she answered.

"Regan, it's Becky. You know, from the comedy club, Larry's Laughs. I'm at a bar, and I just met Chip Jones's roommate."

"His roommate?" Regan asked, astonished.

"Yes! He was leaving. I've been so worried about Chip Jones that I just blurted out, 'You don't know a Chip Jones, do you?' He said yes! Chip's family has been trying to reach him tonight, but he's not answering his cell phone."

"Is his roommate still there?"

"Yes."

"Ask him what college Chip attended."

"Just a sec . . . Chairsworth."

"Where are you?"

"At Lonnie's on Eighty-eighth and Second."

"We're a couple blocks away. Come outside if you would."

Two minutes later, Regan double-parked in front of the bar. Becky was standing on the sidewalk with two young girls who seemed to be her age and a guy who was presumably Chip's roommate. All four occupants of Regan's car scrambled to get out.

"I'm not waiting in here this time," Kit mumbled as she grabbed her crutches. "Me, neither," Billy said as he grabbed her elbow.

Becky made the introductions.

Regan quickly went over everything they'd learned about Georgina, as she handed Phil the ring. He looked distraught. "That's his. Chip told me he wanted to sign up for a comedy class. He made me promise not to tell anyone." He paused for a moment. "Over the years, he's had asthma and sometimes uses an inhaler. He's big and pretty strong but has had respiratory problems. It's bad enough that this wacko could scar him for life, but I'm worried about those knockout drops. If she abandons him—it's already so hard to breathe with this heat and humidity . . ." His voice trailed off.

"I understand," Regan said sympathetically. "We all have to work quickly to find them. We know they were at Sammy's, a bar on Eighty-sixth Street near Third Avenue at some point tonight. It was probably not that long ago. So they may not be far from here. Of course they could be anywhere if they caught a cab or a car service."

"I just called my doorman," Phil said. "Chip definitely hasn't been back to our apartment."

"Do you and Chip have friends you could round up to help look for him? We should cover the parks and the riverbanks and any isolated areas in the city where she might have brought him."

"I'll go back in that bar and make an announcement. This is our new neighborhood joint. I bet a lot of people will help."

"That'd be great. Just be careful what you say. If you slander her, and if for some reason she wasn't responsible for these other incidents, there could be trouble."

"Okay."

"We should let Chip's family know."

Phil winced. "They're already worried about him."

"I'm sure they are," Regan said quietly. "Where do they live?"

"His parents are in Maine and his sister is in San Diego. She works for a news station. I was interviewed on the phone by one of the reporters there about the blackout."

"Let's call his parents first."

Predictably, Sue and Chris Jones started to panic. Regan assured them that they were doing everything they could to find Chip. "The police are on the alert. Phil is calling his friends. We're forming a search party."

"He was always so polite to girls," Sue said, her voice full of pain. "He'd be such an easy mark for a woman like that. And knock-out drops, my God! When I spoke to him, he sounded like he'd had too much to drink."

Sue's husband was on the extension. "We're getting in the car and are on our way down."

"Please be careful," Regan said. "Driving at night like this when you're worried and upset can be very dangerous. And when you hit the areas affected by the blackout the roads will be so dark."

"It'd be worse just sitting here," Chris Jones said firmly. "Now I'm going to call our daughter."

"Tell her not to release any information," Regan warned him. "Please. With any luck the two of them are just out on the town together. She might not have any intention to hurt your son."

"But didn't you say that all of her victims are blond?" Sue asked, her voice cracking.

"I did. But here in New York City it will be harder for her to carry out a crime like this. She doesn't have a car, so maybe she won't even try."

"I pray to God that that's the case," Chris said quietly. "But I don't believe it."

I don't, either, Regan thought. When she hung up, she looked around the group—Phil, Becky, Becky's friends Alexis and Dodie, Kit, and Billy. "We've got to get organized. Phil is going to make an announcement in the bar. We'll ask any volunteers to break into groups and cover different areas. I'll be driving around with—"

"Here comes my dad!" Alexis cried as a Rolls-Royce came down the block. "He'll help. He can drive us around. Becky knows what this lunatic woman looks like!"

Regan turned. The driver of the Rolls pulled up behind her car. She was shocked to see Conrad Spreckles get out from behind the wheel.

"Conrad?"

"Regan?"

"You two know each other?" Alexis shrieked.

"Honey, I sold the loft to Regan and her husband."

"Now I know you're cool," Alexis said to Regan. "My dad's soon-to-be ex-wife loved that place. That's why I was never there. I'm so glad it's not hers anymore."

"Alexis," Conrad gently chided.

I knew something was up when he sold us the loft and Lorraine wasn't around, Regan thought.

"Daddy, I'm so glad you're here," Alexis said as she

162

gave him a hug. "You're just in time. We have to help find someone who could be in a lot of trouble."

"Of course," Conrad responded, a catch in his voice. He felt overcome by the display of affection from his daughter. It had been so long since she'd hugged him like that. Until this moment he didn't realize just how terribly he had missed her. "Regan, I can tell you're in charge here," he managed to say. "What should we do?"

35

The flashing red lights of several parked police cars pierced the darkness on the West Side Highway. "Owww," Wally moaned as a paramedic tended to his nose. "That hurts!"

He and Arthur were still sitting on the ground. Jack Reilly and his assistant, Keith, were crouched down, talking with them. The glass sculptures that had been in the backpack were spread out on the dirty blankets they'd been wrapped in.

Detectives were scouting the surrounding area for the runaway thief.

Arthur's head was spinning. He'd broken into Jack Reilly's apartment tonight, locked his wife on the roof, and now here Reilly was thanking them for their bravery.

Jack patted Arthur on the back. "If you hadn't run after the thief—"

"What about me?" Wally grumbled. "If I hadn't said

a friendly hello to the lunatic, this never would have happened."

Jack laughed. "You're right, Wally. Listen, I'd like for you guys come to my office. I spoke to the owners of the gallery. They are out of their minds with joy. They'll be there, and I know they want to meet you. We have to take these sculptures downtown and lift any prints we can get off of them before they're returned. We'll also lift prints off this grimy backpack and see if it can be traced. I'll get us some food and a new shirt for you, Wally."

"What about my car?"

"Give me the keys. I'll have a couple of my guys get some gas, then drive it to my office."

"Okay."

"We'll want to fingerprint you, Arthur, since we know you touched the sculptures and the backpack. It's called elimination prints. That way we can focus on other prints we pick up."

Arthur felt faint. He'd never been fingerprinted before. Now they'd have a record of his prints. The same prints that were on the stun gun. "Sure," he mumbled. "Wally touched at least one of the sculptures, too."

"Then we'll fingerprint him as well. I'm also planning to get the gallery owners' prints."

Wally and Arthur rode downtown in the back of an unmarked police vehicle. Keith and Jack were in the front. Next time I'll be in handcuffs, Arthur thought miserably.

164

Still clad in their beach attire, the owners of the art gallery were anxiously waiting outside One Police Plaza. Knowing the story would be good publicity for their gallery, they'd contacted the press. Several reporters and photographers who were sick of reporting on people trapped in elevators hurried to the scene. The photographers snapped away as the couple embraced Arthur and the swollen-nosed Wally.

"How can we ever ever thank you?" Leon and Zora Peters cried. "You must come to our opening night reception."

An excited reporter shoved a microphone in Wally's face. "How do you feel?" she asked anxiously.

"My nose is killing me, but I am proud," he said simply. "Proud that we were able to stop a criminal from making off with valuable art that didn't belong to him. I'm sure that the NYPD will have him behind bars in no time. Which is where someone like that should be. And they should throw away the key."

The reporter nodded zealously then turned to Arthur, who was looking at Wally with a shocked expression. "How about you? I understand you were the one who ran after the man who assaulted your friend."

Arthur swallowed. "I'm just so pleased for the gallery owners," he said shakily. "When I went to defend my buddy I had no idea that I'd be helping out people I'd never met . . ."

Leon and Zora Peters were standing next to Arthur, beaming their approval.

After answering a few more questions, they left the

165

reporters and went up to Jack's office where a cele-bratory atmosphere prevailed.

"I'm so glad you did, but what on earth were you doing driving into the city on the night of a blackout?" Leon asked, his eyes widening.

"Um, uh, we thought it would be fun," Arthur stam-mered. "We had heard that there were so many block parties during the last blackout. There was nothing going on where we live in New Jersey."

Leon shrugged. "Sounds like a good reason to me."

"I had just come back from working on a job in Con-necticut," Wally added. "On the way home, the blackout struck. Right after my boss dropped me off, Arthur drove up and said, 'Hey, let's take a ride into the city.' "

So why didn't you just get in Arthur's car? Jack wondered.

A detective popped his head into Jack's office.

"Yes?" Jack said.

The detective held up Arthur's stun gun, which was still in the plastic bag. "We found out this model is sold only on the Internet by a small company that hasn't been in business long. They're based out in Nebraska. It's the cheapest model they make. We should be able to track down who this belongs to. Tomorrow we'll talk to someone from the company."

"Terrific." Jack turned to the others. "My apartment was broken into tonight," he explained. "My wife arrived home when the intruder was there. Luckily she wasn't hurt."

"Oh no!" Zora cried. "That is just awful. All the wolves are out tonight, aren't they?"

"We're lucky that this blackout has been fairly peaceful," Jack said. "But there are wolves out every night."

"Maybe you should enlist the help of these two!" Leon joked, pointing to Wally and Arthur. "Look at what they did for us! And they weren't even trying! Lord knows what they could do if they really put their minds to it!"

Wally and Arthur managed to fake a few hollow laughs.

"My apartment is being renovated, and Wally is on the team doing the work," Jack explained. "That's how he knew to call me tonight when this whole thing happened." He tapped his desk. "By the way, Arthur, what kind of work do you do?"

"Computers," Arthur said quickly. In a rush he added, "That's why I recognized the glass sculptures right away. I'd read the story online . . ."

36

"There's a cab!" Chip shouted as he and Georgina reached Fifth Avenue. He staggered out into the darkened street, waved his arms, and the cab screeched to a halt, narrowly avoiding him. Oblivious to the near miss, Chip opened the back door and jumped in.

"Where are you going?" the driver leaned out the

window and snapped at Georgina. She was standing there, slightly stunned, not having reacted quickly enough to Chip's sudden actions. "This is my last ride of the night," the driver continued. "It's too dangerous out here. It's pitch black and with crazy people like your boyfriend running out into the street, I could have a terrible accident. Tell me where you're going, lady, and get in the car."

In a split second Georgina made her decision. She spat out the address and got in. Chip was leaning back with his eyes closed. The driver took off just as she was shutting the door. Georgina was thankful that he didn't appear to have any interest in more chitchat. The cab had a partition, and the radio was at a high volume, tuned to a news station. An announcer was reporting that city leaders were optimistic that the lights would be back on soon. In the middle of the report, the driver changed the channel to a station playing rock music.

The traffic was light. Most everyone was off the road by now, home roasting in their hot apartments. Tomorrow the city would be full of cranky, tired people, Georgina thought. It took less than ten minutes to reach their destination. The driver stopped and slid open the partition. "Which building?" he asked.

"We'll just get out here at the corner," Georgina answered, glancing at the meter to see what the fare was. She reached through the partition and handed the driver several bills. "That should do it."

"Thanks," the driver mumbled as he snapped the partition shut.

"Come on, Chip," Georgina said, nudging him.

"What?" he asked, his eyes fluttering. "Where are we?"

Georgina opened the door and firmly grabbed hold of his arm. "We're getting out."

"I have to get home," he protested weakly.

"You can't walk up all those flights of stairs," Georgina said breezily, in case the cab driver was paying attention.

She needn't have worried. The cabbie was snapping his fingers, grooving to the music that seemed to be getting louder by the second.

Increasingly stupefied, Chip got out of the car slowly. Everything was dark and quiet. There were no signs of life anywhere. Georgina took his hand. "Come on," she coaxed. "I want to show you something."

"I'm so tired," he muttered as she led him across a street, away from the buildings. "I have to lie down."

"You can lie down in a minute." She walked ahead of him down a grassy knoll, but she held his hand with an iron grip. "It's so nice here. Why would you want to be anywhere else?" She stopped when they reached a stone wall. "Let's settle in behind these bushes. It's nice and private."

"It's so dark," Chip said, stumbling slightly. "It's hard to see anything." He sat down on the ground, laid back, and quickly fell asleep.

Georgina sighed with relief. I really have him here, she thought. Here in the spot I thought I never wanted to be. She stood for several moments, glaring into the darkness, then sat down next to him. Her mind was a jumble of thoughts and emotions. This is where it all happened, and Chip could care less. I'm not good enough for him to worry about. Angrily, she opened her purse and pulled out a pack of cigarettes. She also yanked out the branding tool she planned to use on his arm. That can wait a little while, she thought. I'll smoke my cigarettes. She enjoyed the feeling of being in control of his fate and wanted to savor it. Once she branded him, she'd have to leave right away. But now, if someone happened by and spotted them, there would be nothing to arouse suspicion. They were a young couple escaping the stifling heat of their apartment.

I can't believe I'm here, she kept thinking. I just can't. My life could have been so different. She lit up a cigarette, pulled out her cell phone and turned it on. There were two messages from Paulette, one from Melanie, and one from Dexter. Why were they calling? They didn't want to come to the comedy club tonight. Maybe Kit went back to the hotel and complained to them I'd left her at the club. Too bad. I've been abandoned plenty of times in my life and I've survived.

She didn't want to listen to the messages but was tempted to call Paulette back. Paulette was Georgina's only friend. But she was a mess, too.

No, she decided. I'll call her tomorrow.

Georgina threw the phone back in her purse, and out of curiousity, pulled out Chip's. How very high tech, she thought sarcastically. It was like a miniature computer, complete with a keyboard. She pressed the on button and the phone lit up. I wish I knew how to retrieve his messages, she mused. But without his code, she knew it was hopeless. She tossed the phone on the ground next to her, laid back and took a drag off her cigarette.

As she stared at the stars, which normally weren't so visible above Manhattan, she started to sing. One line of a song. What she didn't know was that when she tossed Chip's phone to the ground, the redial button had been activated.

Chip's parents were hurrying out the door when their phone rang. They both raced back inside. His mother ran to the kitchen and his father to the living room. "It's Chip," his mother screamed when she saw the number on the caller ID. She and her husband answered at once.

"Hello, Chip!" they cried, their voices hopeful. "Chip!"

But there was no response. All they could hear was the faint sound of a woman singing.

"Chip!" they called. "Chip, please talk to us!"

A puzzled expression came over Georgina's face. "What is that noise?" she muttered, then glanced over at Chip's phone. Picking it up and holding it to her ear, she could hear a man and a woman speaking into the phone.

"Chip, this is Mom—and Dad. Where are you?"

Georgina pressed the disconnect button. Now she

was really angry. Those were two people who would never approve of her. She was sure of it. They wouldn't be inviting her to Maine for a nice long weekend of lobster and white wine. "He's here," she said aloud as she made sure the phone was switched off. "But he can't talk to you right now." She then laughed bitterly. "He may never talk to you again."

She lay back down and resumed smoking her cigarette. It made her feel a little bit better. Life was so unfair, she thought. I've never gotten a break. Not like this privileged brat lying next to me. He has two parents who love him. The sound of their worried voices made her so angry. No one on this planet feels that way about me, she thought.

Chip was in a dead sleep. He was so quiet and still, she leaned over to make sure he was breathing.

He was.

37

The crowd of young people outside Lonnie's bar was growing by the minute. Phil had gone inside to make the announcement about forming a search party, and the bar had practically emptied out. Almost everyone was on a cell phone, trying to get in touch with friends, asking them to come down from their apartments and bring flashlights.

"When something like this happens we all realize it could have easily been one of us," a petite girl with a dark tan said quietly to Regan. "I feel terrible. It's just usually a girl who disappears, not a guy."

"I know," Regan said. She called out to the crowd. "If everyone could listen for a minute. First of all, we really appreciate your help. Chip Jones's parents are on their way down from Maine and they are frantic. The bartender here at Lonnie's, Josh Gaspero, offered to stay open so we can use the bar as a base. I know cell phone service is spotty. But please take the number of the landline at the bar and try to periodically check in. Josh will be notified right away if there is any news. Also be sure to get my number and Phil's number. We want to pass the word as quickly as possible if there are any developments. Write your names and numbers on the sheet of paper Josh has at the bar so that we can keep track of everyone. You know we have to look in isolated areas, so please, don't walk around alone. Break up into groups."

"There are seven or eight of us who will go into Central Park together," one guy called out.

"Great," Regan said. "I think a good plan would be for the rest of you to focus on the Upper East Side. Go down by the river and Carl Schurz Park. If any of your friends show up with cars, you can fan out to other areas." Regan's cell phone rang. "Excuse me. I think it's Chip's parents," she said. She turned away and answered.

"Regan, someone just called from Chip's cell phone," Chris Jones said, his voice clipped. Regan could hear Sue crying on the extension.

"What did they say?"

"All we could hear was a woman singing, almost to herself. Then she stopped. A moment later the phone was disconnected. We tried to call back and it went right to his voice mail."

"Singing? What was she singing?"

"Only the good die young," Sue answered, her voice hysterical. "She kept singing that one line over and over."

Regan's heart skipped a beat. "Could you hear anything else in the background?"

"I think I heard a car honk its horn. There was also the distant sound of a police siren."

"You think they were calling from outside?"

"Either that or they were sitting next to an open window. Why would someone do this to us?" Sue demanded. "Why would she taunt us like that? How would she even know our number?"

"Chip probably has it programmed in his phone," Regan answered. "You said you spoke to him tonight. Did you call him?"

"Yes," Sue answered. "We called him as soon as we heard about the blackout."

"But, honey, remember, he called us back because the connection was bad," Chris reminded her.

"If that was the case, and you were the last one he called, his phone might have accidentally hit redial. Does he have one of those high tech phones that don't fold over?"

"Yes."

"A friend of mine recently ended up with a conversation recorded on her answering machine that the person who left it certainly never intended her to hear. He had just left her a message and didn't realize it when his phone hit redial. The same thing could have happened here."

"But his phone had been turned off. And why was she singing that song?" Sue demanded.

"I don't know but I'll call the detective in Atlanta who has Georgina's friend in custody. This friend is willing to give any information she can to save her own skin. Maybe this song will have some significance. We're trying to figure out if there's someplace in the city that has special meaning to Georgina where she may have gone."

"If she has his phone and he didn't talk to us, it must mean that he's already drugged—" Sue began.

"Don't go there," Regan warned her. "We have a lot of people about to hit the streets looking for your son, and the police have been notified."

"We're getting in the car now," Chris said quickly. "I'm putting our phone on call forwarding in case they call back. Keep in touch with us. Regan, please find him."

When she hung up, Regan called Detective McFadden in Atlanta and asked him to find out about the song and to ask Paulette if she knew where Georgina's grandmother had lived. Paulette had never heard Georgina mention the song, but she did remember that the grandmother had lived somewhere on the Lower East Side. She didn't have a specific address.

Regan got the crowd's attention again and told them of the phone call Chip's parents had received. "We've got to move fast. Chip might already be drugged. Remember, safety in numbers. Please be careful."

Regan turned to Conrad who was standing with Kit, Alexis, Becky, Dodie, and Phil.

"Where do you want us to go?" Conrad asked.

"Let's see. Phil's friends are covering the Upper East Side . . ."

Phil nodded. "Dodie and I will also stay around here. I know this area and will be keeping in close touch with Josh. I don't want the search parties to lose any momentum if in a couple of hours—" He stopped speaking, unable to continue.

"That's a great idea, Phil," Regan said quickly. "Conrad, why don't you drive Becky and Alexis around Tribeca? I know you're familiar with that part of the city. There are a lot of isolated areas down by the river where they could be. My group will cover the Lower East Side. That's where Georgina's grandmother lived. Maybe she took Chip for a stroll down memory lane."

"Of course, Regan." Conrad started toward his car, then turned back and grabbed Regan's hand. "I can only imagine how his parents must feel. We'll drive around all night until we find him."

"Thanks, Conrad. By the way, you have a lovely daughter."

He smiled. "I know. I'm very lucky."

As they got into their cars, Regan kept having the same thought. If Georgina planned to pull this same crime off in Manhattan tonight, without a car, then she must have had some location in mind. She couldn't just drive around looking for a perfect spot like she could in the other cities. But where in Manhattan could it be?

And why did she choose it?

38

Rod, the contractor, and his wife, Lee, were sitting at the patio table on the deck he'd built right outside their kitchen. The kids were in bed, and they were enjoying a quiet drink. An old transistor radio with its volume turned down was between them. They'd listened on and off to updates about the blackout.

"Keep your fingers crossed," Rod said. "If the blackout lasts through tomorrow morning, I don't have to give the Reillys an excuse for not showing up until Wednesday."

Lee, a bouncy, vibrant woman laughed. "I don't know how you do all that juggling. My stomach would be in knots."

"Don't worry, my sweet," Rod said with a casual wave of his hand. "They all love me in the end." Hearing the music that preceded breaking news, he turned up the volume on the radio.

"And now," a male announcer proclaimed, "we have

a special report from outside One Police Plaza. What have you got for us, Gina?"

"What we've got is a lucky break for the Major Case Squad. A gallery in SoHo was broken into when the blackout struck, and valuable glass sculptures were stolen. Two men who ran out of gas on the West Side Highway were walking along the path next to the river when they had a run-in with the thief and unwittingly recovered the art. The men are both from New Jersey. A Wally Madison and Arthur—"

"What?" Rod yelled as he grabbed the radio.

"We caught up with the heroes outside One Police Plaza. The head of the Major Case Squad, Jack Reilly, was taking them up to his office, along with the owners of the art gallery. Needless to say, they're all thrilled. I have an unconfirmed report that Jack Reilly's apartment was also broken into tonight. As far as we know, nothing was taken."

"What was Wally doing in New York City?" Rod yelped. His cool and calm demeanor had quickly headed south.

"Reilly's wife walked in right before the blackout struck. The intruder was in the apartment, locked her outside on the roof, and made his escape. We'll keep you updated."

"Dear God," Rod said. "Someone broke into their apartment. That's terrible."

"It is. But Jack Reilly's happy Wally recovered the stolen sculptures. That can only be good for you," Lee said practically.

"We had a long day today and we're going to have a long day tomorrow. I'm surprised Wally went out so late. He seemed a little edgy tonight. Let me call him."

Rod went into the kitchen and picked up the phone. He couldn't get through on Wally's cell phone, so he decided to call Jack Reilly's office.

"My word!" Rod exclaimed when he got Jack on the phone. "I just heard on the radio about everything that's going on with Wally. It's unbelievable. And I'm so sorry about your apartment."

"Word spreads fast. Thankfully Regan is okay and that's what counts."

"How did they get in?"

"There was no sign of forced entry. They must have had a key."

"Jack, I can assure you I've kept control of the keys. Wally and Frank and I were in the van on the way home from Connecticut when the blackout struck."

"Rod, don't worry. We never changed the locks when we bought the loft from Conrad Spreckles. It could have been someone he knew who had a key. Anything's possible. We didn't think it was important to replace the keys right away because the apartments weren't connected and there was nothing to steal in the new one. As soon as you broke down the wall, we should have had new keys made. We'll take care of that first thing in the morning."

At that moment, the lights flickered back on in Rod's kitchen. He gasped as his stomach fell six feet.

"Are you all right?"

179

"Yes, just a bit surprised. The lights are coming back on in my house."

"Fantastic!" Jack said. "Let's hope they're back on everywhere before long. Do you want to talk to Wally? We're about to head out. He's going to help us out tonight with another case. Regan is trying to locate a young guy who's on the town with a woman who is a predator. The poor kid doesn't know what he's in for. Wally and his friend Arthur offered to join the search party."

"I'd like to help," Rod volunteered.

"That's nice of you, Rod, but if you're out in New Jersey—"

"I'll come in right now. The electricity is back on here so I don't have to worry about my family. I'll just talk to Wally for a second."

"Sure. Here he is."

Rod waited while Jack handed over the phone.

"Hello," Wally said, sounding quite nasal.

"Wally—you're a hero."

"My nose is crooked but we made a lot of people happy tonight. Now there's a much more serious situation—"

"I'm coming in. I want to help, too."

"Are you sure?"

"Yes."

"Conrad Spreckles is out looking for this guy, too."

"What?"

"It's a long story. Regan just called Jack and told him. Conrad's daughter was at a bar in New York and got involved with the whole thing."

"Where can I meet you?"

"We've been assigned to the Upper West Side. That's where we're going in a few minutes."

"I'm leaving now. I'll call you when I get close and we'll figure out exactly where to meet."

Rod hung up. He did want to help. But he also had a funny feeling about the break-in at the Reillys. If Jack Reilly suspected any of them, he wasn't letting on. Rod wanted to see who this friend of Wally's was. Wally had seemed disturbed when he learned the Reillys expected them back tomorrow, not Wednesday. But no matter what happened, Rod wanted it to be clear that he was a trustworthy man. Except, of course, about showing up when promised.

Rod turned. Lee was standing there staring at him. "My dear, for someone who lets everything roll off his back, you look a little worried."

39

"According to Cal, this is the address of the bar where Georgina's grandmother worked," Regan said as she stopped the car in front of what was now a health food restaurant. It was locked up tight, with large metal gates in front of the windows.

"And from what he said about her grandmother, she must be rolling in her grave," Billy commented.

Regan sighed. "It must have been a tremendous loss

for Georgina when her grandmother died."

Melanie nodded. "It seemed that way when she told me about her."

"I wonder if Georgina's been back to New York since then."

"I don't know," Melanie answered. "When we were flying up here, I asked if she'd ever been to New York. She said yes but not in years. She never said a word about her grandmother having lived here."

Regan sighed. She glanced around the dark and quiet street. "I don't think there's anyplace around here Georgina could have dragged poor Chip. Since we're following her grandmother's footsteps, let's try the Lower East Side." She flipped on the radio.

"Lights have come back on in sections of New Jersey," an announcer said excitedly. "That means people can get out of bed and turn on the air conditioner—"

"If the lights came back on in Manhattan, it would certainly help," Regan commented.

Kit leaned forward. "I was in one of the seminars with Georgina today. She seemed normal enough but was quiet and didn't ask questions. But then after she'd had a drink at the cocktail party she was more aggressive. On the way over to the comedy club it seemed like she was getting a little manic."

"And if she kept on drinking who knows what her state of mind is now," Regan said.

Below Fourteenth Street, on the Lower East Side, they slowly rode up and down the streets. On Second

Street between First and Second Avenues they discovered an old cemetery that took up about half the block and was protected from intruders by a tall black wrought-iron fence. The entrance was chained shut.

"This is the kind of isolated place where Georgina would want to be with Chip," Regan said as she stopped the car.

"I was thinking about doing some jokes about a guy who visits a cemetery," Billy said, "and I started to do some research. A law was passed in 1852 that made it illegal to bury a body in Manhattan. This is one of the only cemeteries left and it's landmarked."

"My father's a funeral director in New Jersey," Regan said. "I didn't know that."

"They passed the law after two cholera epidemics—one in the early 1830s and the second in 1849. So many people in Manhattan died that they were running out of land to bury the dead. People were also afraid that the drinking water was being diseased by water that washed down from the gravesites. They passed the law and actually exhumed thousands of skeletons from Manhattan and moved them out to Queens where the cemetery business was just getting started. For the first time you had to pay to bury your loved ones. So many cemeteries were opened in western Queens that it became known as the Cemetery Belt."

Kit just looked at him. "Really?"

"Don't worry. I didn't make any jokes about it. It's amazing what you can discover online."

"I wonder if Georgina's grandmother is buried in Queens," Regan mused.

"If she was, do you think Georgina might have taken Chip out there?" Kit asked.

"Highly unlikely," Regan answered. "First she'd have to get a car or cab to take them out and drop them off near the cemetery, since she can't exactly say that's where they were going. I doubt she'd find any driver interested in taking the trip during this blackout. Second, I don't think Chip would have left Manhattan willingly. If he were already knocked out, any driver she might have found should have gotten suspicious."

"That reminds me of a story!" Kit exclaimed.

"I think I know the one," Regan said, raising her eyebrows.

"A woman met a guy online," Kit continued for the benefit of Billy and Melanie. "They had a date that must have gone well. He told her he wanted to introduce her to his parents. She agreed. So one night he picked her up for what she thought was going to be a pleasant dinner with Mom and Pop. He drove her to their gravesite."

"Meet the parents!" Billy cried.

Melanie's mouth had dropped open. "That is really weird."

"Don't tell me. There was no third date," Billy said.

"I don't think so," Kit answered, shaking her head.

Regan put the car into drive and slowly moved it forward. "Let's go down by the East River and make our way around the tip of Manhattan. If Chip is already drugged, she wouldn't be with him on the streets." She then stopped the car.

"What's the matter?" Kit asked.

"I'm going to call that detective in Atlanta and ask him to find out everything Georgina might have told Paulette about her grandmother. Maybe there was a special place in the city they used to go together. Maybe they sat by the river somewhere and watched the boats go by. I can't believe that wherever she brought Chip tonight doesn't have some significance." As Regan put the call through, she couldn't get the line of the song out of her head.

Only the good die young.

40

Lorraine, impatiently waiting on the park bench across from the Treetops Hotel, finally spotted Clay about to go through its front door. She jumped up and started to run across Central Park South. "Clay!"

He stopped and turned. The greeter spotted him and started to open the door of the hotel, a big smile plastered on his face.

"Let's get away from here!" Lorraine growled.

But it was too late. "Miss Lily!" the greeter said effusively. "Welcome back! There is a radio reporter on the phone speaking to the front desk manager. He had asked to speak to you. He saw you on television before—"

Clay just looked at her. "You were on television before?"

Lorraine fluffed up her hair. "There was a camera crew when I checked in. I'll be right back."

Ten minutes later she reappeared. They started down the block, heading west. "What took you so long?" she snapped. "And where is your bicycle?"

"Me! You're stopping for interviews."

"How could I refuse? The hotel just lent me these ugly shoes."

He looked down. "I won't disagree with you on that."

Lorraine ignored the remark. "So what happened?"

"I tried to call you."

"The battery on my phone is dead."

Clay rolled his eyes. "My roommate's girlfriend borrowed my bicycle and got a flat tire. I could kill her. I'm so sick of those two. I borrowed a pair of her tap shoes. They were in the bathroom. I thought they'd fit you."

"Oh sure. Tap shoes. Just what I need to wear when we're sneaking up the stairwell. Why don't you borrow a pair in your size, and we can pretend we're Fred and Ginger?"

"I'm doing my best, Lorraine. You didn't give me much notice about this job. I also grabbed some of my tools in case your key doesn't work."

"Well, that's good." At the corner of Sixth Avenue and Central Park South, Lorraine turned her head to the right. The sight of a familiar vehicle caught her eye as it was briefly illuminated by the headlights of an oncoming car. "Oh no!" she cried, and pulled Clay to make the turn down Sixth.

"What's wrong?"

"That was Conrad's Rolls-Royce at the corner. He was heading west."

"Are you sure?"

"Yes! He's driving. When I spoke to him earlier he was in Connecticut. He must be spying on me."

"He doesn't need to spy on you. You've been on TV and the radio tonight! Live from the Treetops Hotel! I'm sure the Candy Man didn't predict you'd go out for a walk."

"Do you think he's going down to the loft because they discovered the safe?" Lorraine asked in a panicked voice.

"Now you're getting paranoid."

"What else would he be doing here?"

"How am I supposed to know? You're the one who's married to him."

"Not for much longer. And if he gets his hands on those letters, it'll make his day and ruin my life!"

"All right then. We're both freshly motivated to get this job done. I want the money for my own apartment, and you want the letters back. Let's go."

"What if the Reillys are home by now?"

Clay pulled out his cell phone. "I'll call them again." He looked up recently dialed numbers and pressed the Reillys'. The connection was made and their phone began to ring. And ring and ring. "Music to my ears," he said. "I bet they're both out fighting crime."

"I wish we could find a cab," Lorraine whined.

But Sixth Avenue was pitch dark. There wasn't a car in sight.

"The longest journey begins with a single step," Clay pronounced as he offered Lorraine his arm. "Let's go."

41

Conrad had decided to drive across Central Park South on their way to Tribeca. The fact that they were passing the Treetops Hotel did not go unnoticed by his daughter. As they crossed the intersection at Sixth Avenue, Alexis screeched, "Daddy! I think I just saw Lorraine!"

"Where?" Conrad's head almost spun around.

"Back on the corner of Sixth Avenue with some guy. It's so dark it's hard to tell. The lights of a passing car made them visible for about a second. They turned and went down Sixth Avenue."

"Could be," Conrad said, wondering who the guy was. "She's staying right there at the Treetops. I can't imagine why she'd be out for a stroll at this time of night when she's staying in a luxurious air-conditioned hotel."

Alexis shrugged. "I'm so glad you're getting rid of her."

Conrad patted his daughter's hand. "Let's not worry about Lorraine right now. Chip Jones is our concern."

"I've got my eyes peeled," Becky piped up from the back seat.

"So do I!" Alexis said. "How else would I have spotted that no good—"

"Alexis."

"Sorry, Dad. But maybe it's a good sign. If I can spot Lorraine during this blackout, then maybe the wretch who's with Chip Jones will also be discovered."

"I certainly hope so."

"And they both should be locked up."

42

After taking Regan's call, Detective McFadden returned to the interrogation room where twenty-five-year-old Paulette Dobson was sitting at a table, her head in her hands. She was exhausted, upset, but most of all petrified. Small-boned with stringy light brown hair that needed a trim, she had a waifish quality. Her skin and eyes were pale, her features plain.

"I want to help in whatever way I can," she said yet again, struggling to sit up straight when McFadden reappeared. "I'm so sorry I didn't report her right away. But she just told me about this the other night."

Over the course of the evening, Paulette had recounted her history with Georgina. They'd met three years ago when they were both waitresses at a diner outside Atlanta and had gotten friendly during their cigarette breaks. They'd started hanging out at bars and often went shopping together. One day when they were driving home from the mall, Georgina pulled a blouse out of her oversized purse that she had stolen from one of the stores. Paulette couldn't believe it. Georgina convinced her it was easy, she had to try it herself, and when Paulette was successful at her first attempt, it became a game for them. But when Georgina had several days off in a row, she'd get in her car and go away alone. She'd told Paulette that she was so used to being a loner, there were times when she needed to be by herself. Two nights ago, after a day of heavy shoplifting, and an evening of even heavier drinking, Paulette and Georgina were in Georgina's apartment admiring all their loot. It was then that Georgina excitedly told Paulette what she did on those trips.

"When she showed me the brand she used to burn the guys' skin, I felt sick," Paulette had said.

"You knew she was going on another trip but you didn't report her until we tracked you down today on the shoplifting charges," McFadden responded.

"I wanted to! And I would have. But I was so scared. I've been a wreck since Saturday night. I've barely slept. How can I call the police when Georgina's got all these clothes we stole in her apartment, some with the security tags still on them?" Paulette paused to catch her breath. "She had this new job. She was so surprised that they hired her because she'd lied so much on her application and résumé. She told me she didn't have any business experience so she had to make up places she'd supposedly worked at before. Her new company must not have checked out any of it. Anyway, since it was a business trip I was hoping she'd be with the people from her company and wouldn't do anything bad. But she can be so unpredictable. Sometimes she was so much fun and would be laughing really hard and other times she got really scary and mean. I couldn't even be sure what she told me about the guys was true, because she can be such a liar, and I had no proof, but now that they've found the pictures, I don't know why she didn't show them to me."

"They've found pictures, and the young man she is with is in terrible danger."

"I know," Paulette whimpered. "It's my fault. I should have called the police. I knew I'd end up in big trouble, but I was even more scared of Georgina getting revenge. I don't care about that anymore." She put her hands up to her face as if to protect herself from pain. "I was also afraid because I'd told her about things that had happened in my life that were very personal. Things that I would never want anyone else to know. You take a big risk when you confide your secrets to people."

McFadden was amused that she didn't even get the irony of what she was saying. But this Paulette was clearly a follower. A naïve follower. Big, bad Georgina had come into her life and taken over.

Now as McFadden sat down again across the table from Paulette, he looked at her kindly. "Georgina's grandmother lived in New York. That fact didn't come up until my colleague in New York asked me to find out if you knew anything about her. You didn't think it was important to mention her when we first started talking tonight?"

Paulette blinked. "No. We'd been talking about what she did to the guys she picked up and her ex-boyfriend, Huck. She was obsessed by him."

"Did Georgina mention any special places she went with her grandmother on her visits to New York?"

"No. There was only one night when she really talked to me about her grandmother."

"When was that?"

"It wasn't long after we met. One night a lady came into the diner. Georgina's eyes got all watery. I'd never seen her like that before. She rushed into the ladies room, and I followed her to see if she was okay. Turns out that the woman looked so much like Georgina's grandmother, it was really upsetting for her. She was trying so hard not to cry but she said the sight of that woman brought all her sadness to the surface. I told her I'd take her out for a drink after we got off work. We went to a bar, sat in the corner, and she poured her heart out, as much as someone like Georgina would, about her grandmother. That's when we got close."

McFadden waited.

"When Georgina was a baby, her father died. Her

mother lived with different guys, and they moved around a lot. Georgina's paternal grandmother lived in New York City. She said she loved to go visit her, and wanted to live with her, but Georgina's mother wouldn't allow it. She still liked to think of herself as a mother even though she pretty much ignored Georgina. But her grandmother doted on her. She took her on trips. They were going on vacation together and that's when the grandmother died in a car accident. I think Georgina felt responsible. After that night in the bar, Georgina didn't talk about her grandmother to me again. If I brought the subject up, she brushed me off. It was almost like she was embarrassed that she'd been so open."

"Was Georgina in the car with her grandmother when she died?"

"No."

"But they were on vacation together?"

Paulette looked slightly exasperated. "They weren't *on* vacation together. They were *going* on vacation together. Her grandmother was in a cab on the way to the airport when the accident happened. She was planning to arrive in Miami first and meet Georgina's flight when it came in. It was before cell phones, so by the time Georgina's mother heard about the accident, Georgina was in Miami with someone from the airline, waiting for her grandmother to pick her up."

There was silence in the room for a moment. "One of Georgina's victims was a young man she met at a comedy club in Miami," McFadden said.

"That's right."

"Did she say why she chose that particular city?"

"No. She told me she drove to places where she knew there were good comedy clubs. Her grandmother loved comedies and they used to go to the movies a lot."

"If her grandmother died in a cab on the way to the airport, then the accident took place in New York?"

"Yes. She was thrown from the cab and hurled over the side of the highway. Georgina said she was killed instantly."

"Do you know where in New York this happened?"

"No. She didn't say. I've never been there so the exact location wouldn't have meant anything to me. The only place I do remember Georgina mentioning is the Lower East Side, where she said her grandmother lived." Paulette paused. "Do you think where her grandmother died is important?"

"It could very well be. People often place flowers on the side of the road at the spot where loved ones died in car accidents." He started to get out of his chair. "I'm sure you've seen them on your trips to the mall," he added sharply. "Perhaps Georgina isn't interested as much in placing flowers at the location where her grandmother died as she is in carrying out her vicious assault there. I'll phone my colleague in New York. She was under the impression the accident took place out of town."

"That stupid Huck!" Paulette cried. "I wish we knew where he was so you could talk to him."

"Why?"

"Georgina said that he had told her he wanted to take her to New York and be with her the first time she visited since her grandmother died. He promised to take her to the accident site. He fed her all the lines, saying he wanted to take care of her and make her happy again. He grew up somewhere near New York, so if anyone knows where the accident took place, it would be him." She wiped her eyes. "He dumped Georgina for her roommate. It can't get much worse than that."

"He grew up near New York?"

"Yes."

"What was his full name?"

"Huckleberry Darling. Can you imagine? A creep like that has a last name like Darling?"

McFadden hurriedly left the room and called Regan.

43

Regan's search party wasn't far from One Police Plaza when McFadden called back and filled her in. ". . . and Paulette is sure that this guy Huck Darling would know where the accident happened. She said that Georgina could never track him down. Lucky for him, I guess. How many Huckleberry Darlings can there be in this world?"

"One is all we need," Regan answered. When she hung up, she called the head of security at the Gates

Hotel. "Cal, it turns out Georgina's grandmother's accident happened here in New York City."

"It did?" he asked, surprise in his voice.

"Yes."

"I had a job in California for a couple of years. I heard about the accident but as I told you, I thought it was when she was on vacation."

"Actually she was in a cab on the way to the airport, *going* on vacation. Do you by any chance remember what her name was? We could do a search on the Internet and see if there was anything written about the accident. If Georgina is twenty-seven now, and she was twelve when her grandmother died, it would have been fifteen years ago."

"I don't know what her name was. Not even her real first name. Everyone called her Alice."

"Why?"

"She loved *The Honeymooners* show and had the same kind of personality as Ralph Kramden's wife. There was a television on the wall in the corner behind the bar, usually tuned to a sports station. At the same time every night she'd change the channel to catch one of the old reruns. Once she started to switch stations when we were watching a big basketball game that had gone into overtime. The guys at the bar went into such an uproar that she switched it back. It was so funny. I think she was just playing with us. Our team lost, and she couldn't have been happier. She was something else. We had some good times with her."

For a moment Regan imagined what it must have

been like when the twelve-year-old Georgina, anxiously waiting for her larger-than-life, beloved grandmother to pick her up at the Miami Airport, was told that she had been killed. Killed on a highway in New York City. "Maybe Alice had the same last name as Georgina," Regan said. "She was Georgina's father's mother."

"They could have the same last name, but I doubt it. Alice joked that after having been married three times, she'd sworn off men."

"Okay, Cal. If you think of someone who might know where the accident took place, or what Alice's real name was, please call them. I have a strong hunch that Georgina might very well visit the scene of the accident tonight. The detective in Atlanta feels the same way."

"I'll see if I can get in touch with a couple of my buddies from back then."

When Regan hung up, she called Jack. "We're right near your office. I'd like to come up for a few minutes. I have new information from the detective in Atlanta. We need to regroup."

"Sure. I'll tell the security guard downstairs you're coming. Wally's here in my office along with other people who want to meet you and help with the search for Chip Jones."

Six minutes later, Regan and her crew were hurrying down the hall to Jack's office. Kit was keeping up on her crutches, Billy at her side.

Regan said a quick hello to the detectives working at

their desks in the outer area. "How's it going?" she asked.

"Okay, Regan. We've got officers all over the city on the alert for Chip Jones."

Regan nodded. "Thanks."

In Jack's corner office, the gallery owners were bursting with good will. "We were blessed tonight," Zora said intensely, as she and Leon rushed to meet Regan. "Now we want to help you." She grabbed Regan's hand and stared soulfully into her eyes. Leon grabbed Regan's other hand and waved it back and forth.

"Thank you." Regan said, nodding her head and extricating herself as politely as possible from their grasp. She leaned over Jack's desk to give him a quick hug. Both knew what the other was thinking.

More introductions were made as Kit and Melanie and Billy entered the room. A seat was quickly produced for Kit. When Regan shook Arthur's hand, she thought it felt unusually sweaty. His demeanor didn't suggest that of someone being feted for his heroism. Maybe he's just shy, she thought. Wally seemed like the same old Wally, except for his swollen nose.

"I know Jack has told you what's going on," Regan began. "We have people searching the city for Chip Jones and this woman Georgina." She quickly told them what she knew about Georgina's past, her ex-boyfriend, Huck Darling, and her grandmother's accident. "I'd like for us to cover the highways leading from the city to the three major airports. Other groups are looking in places like Central Park and Tribeca. Georgina could be anywhere, but I have the strong feeling that wherever the accident happened, is where she went tonight. I could be completely in left field, but for now this is what I'd like to focus on. But before we leave I want to see if we can quickly track down any information about Huck Darling. It would be a miracle if we could get in touch with him."

Arthur, who was a quivering wreck, started to speak. At first nothing would come out of his mouth. Meeting Jack Reilly was stressful enough. But he couldn't believe that Regan Reilly, the woman standing right next to him, was the person he'd locked out on a rooftop tonight. I have to function without falling apart, he told himself. Maybe if I help out with two criminal cases tonight, I'll get a lesser prison sentence for breaking and entering.

Regan looked at him. "Did you want to say something?"

"I'm—I'm—I'm a computer person."

Wally got irritated. "So what, Arthur, she doesn't care about that now."

"Let him talk, Wally," Regan said.

"What I mean is, I've managed to track down friends of friends through the Internet. Honestly, I love it. Those search engines are great, but if you can't find something easily, I know how to keep looking. I'm sorry. I'm sure there are plenty of people in this building who could do a better job of it. I just thought . . ."

"We can use all the help we can get," Regan said.

"If anyone can do it Arthur can," Zora cried, as if she'd known him for a lifetime. "Thanks to him we have our sculptures back."

"Me, too." Wally said indignantly.

"Of course you, too, I'm so sorry," Zora gushed. "But Arthur grabbed the backpack full of our precious babies."

Another loon, Regan thought as Jack got up from his desk. "Arthur, sit right here at my computer. It's all yours."

Arthur jumped up and hurried over. "You said his name was Huck Darling and that he grew up somewhere around New York City? He'd be in his late twenties?"

"Yes, and Huck is short for Huckleberry."

Arthur raised his eyebrows. "That can only be good for us," he muttered as he sat down in front of the keyboard. Regan noticed an instant change in his bearing. As his fingers started flying over the keyboard, he looked confident and in control. Let's hope he finds something, she thought, then turned to Melanie. "Would you call Dexter and see if Georgina put the name of a college on her job application? I know she lied about previous employment, but we need to help Arthur with any leads we can. Paulette didn't know the name of the college, and Georgina dropped out anyway. But if she did list the college where she met Huck, and it's his alma mater, it might help."

"Sure, Regan." Melanie pulled out her cell phone,

pressed in Dexter's number, and stepped outside the office.

"Regan, I'll drive anywhere you want looking for them," Wally offered, feeling left out that Arthur was getting all the attention. "East, west, north, south . . ."

"I appreciate that, Wally," Regan answered. She turned to the map on Jack's wall. "Let's take a look at this. It covers the entire city of New York," she began.

A moment later, Melanie burst back into the room. "Dexter spoke with our company president a little while ago. He's so mad. Among other lies, Georgina made up the name of the college on her application. Dexter is in so much trouble. I can't believe he hired her without checking on *anything!*"

"Thanks, Melanie," Regan said. Dexter will be filling out his own job applications soon, she thought. "We were just about to go over this map and decide what highways—"

"Oh, my Darling!" Arthur whooped. "Oh, my Darling!"

"Arthur, what is it?" Regan asked.

"Georgina is really going to have a fit when she hears this one!"

"What?"

"He's right here! Huck Darling just moved to New York City. I found the records. He purchased an apartment at the Schwab House on Seventy-fourth Street and West End Avenue. He must have some serious dough."

"Is there a phone number?" Regan asked quickly.

"There's no listing."

"Does he have a cell phone?" Wally asked.

Arthur looked aghast. "What do you want from me, Wally? I'm not Ma Bell."

Wally shrugged.

Regan looked at Jack. "Let's go up there now," she said urgently.

"We'll ride in my car with Kit, Billy, and Melanie," Jack answered. "Wally and Arthur and Leon and Zora can ride in Wally's car." He turned to them. "Meet us up there?"

But he didn't wait for an answer from anyone.

Within seconds, Jack's office was empty.

They were all racing to get to the Upper West Side of Manhattan as soon as possible, hoping against hope that Huckleberry Darling would be in residence.

He's our only chance, Regan thought anxiously as the police vehicle, siren blaring and lights flashing, sped through a pitch-black Manhattan.

44

Phil and Dodie walked down Eighty-eighth Street to East End Avenue and entered Carl Schurz Park. Once the private garden of Gracie Mansion, the official residence of the mayor of the city of New York, it was now a fourteen-acre neighborhood oasis, with beautiful views of the East River and the surrounding bridges. As Phil and Dodie followed the park's winding paths, they scanned the landscape with their flashlights. The only people they encountered were out strolling with their dogs.

"They're not here," Phil finally said. "Let's head up toward Central Park. I'd like to stop by Lonnie's first and see if there are any more people who might want to join us."

"Sure."

As they walked along, saying nothing, Dodie finally felt compelled to break the silence. "How are you doing?"

"Not so well."

"Sorry. It was a stupid question."

"Don't be sorry. I just can't stop thinking about Chip. He is such a good guy. I just know he's never been mean to a girl. In fact, he's polite to a fault. If any guy doesn't deserve having a woman taking out her frustrations on him, it's Chip." Phil shuddered. "I can't imagine having a brand like that on my arm for the rest of my life. But if she slipped him a drug his body can't handle . . ."

The sound of happy, vibrant mambo music interrupted him. It was the ring Phil had chosen for his cell phone, but at this moment it frayed his nerves. He pulled the phone off his belt and answered quickly. Chip's sister, Natalie, was calling from San Diego. Understandably, she was a wreck.

"Phil, is there any news?" she asked, her voice quivering.

"No, Natalie. We're out looking for Chip right now."

"I wish I could get on a plane, but there are no flights to New York. I've been researching knockout drops. They are very dangerous if you have respiratory problems. Do you remember last year when Chip had walking pneumonia? It was really bad."

"Yes," Phil answered, his voice tight.

"And he's just getting over a cold. He was still coughing when I talked to him yesterday."

"Natalie, we're going to find him," Phil said, forcing optimism into his voice.

"My parents are driving down to the city. I'm so worried about them, too. They're upset and it's late and the roads are dark."

"They insisted."

"I don't blame them, I'd do the same. But please, Phil, call me back soon. Even if there's nothing new. Sitting here waiting for the phone to ring is torture."

"I promise, Natalie."

She started to cry. "He's my little brother. He needs my help, and I can't be there for him."

"Oh, Natalie. He loves you so much. He's always talking about how good you are to him."

"He is?"

"Yes. Don't worry, he'll be okay."

"I don't know who this girl is," Natalie said vehemently, "but if I ever get my hands on her . . ."

"How about this?" Phil asked, trying to lighten the tone of the conversation. "When we catch her, I'll personally arrange a meeting between you. We'll put you in the ring together. She won't stand a chance."

"You're damned right she won't stand a chance. I won't need any knockout drops. One punch is all it'll take!"

"That's the spirit. I'll call you back soon." When he hung up the phone, his face crumbled. He grabbed Dodie's hand. "We've got to walk faster. I've got the feeling we're running out of time . . ."

45

Georgina decided to smoke one last cigarette before she got to work. She tapped Chip on the shoulder. He didn't move. Out cold and down for the count, she thought. Well, that's good. I don't need for him to wake up, screaming in pain. Her thoughts drifted. She was oblivious to the sound of the cars on the highway above. Fifteen years. Fifteen years since some stupid driver got distracted by the sight of a cruise ship and lost control of his car. The vehicle jumped the divider and slammed into Nana's cab. She was on her way to Newark airport. We were going to have such a wonderful vacation together. Georgina glanced up at that very highway with tears in her eyes.

So many things happen by chance, Georgina thought bitterly as she lit her cigarette. She inhaled, then sat up. Huck only got to know her roommate because he spent so much time hanging around their dorm room. At first, he'd told Georgina he "didn't take to that girl." So if she hadn't been Georgina's roommate, then he never would have realized that in fact, he *did* "take to that girl" quite a bit. And here I am for the first time in the sacred place that he promised to visit with me. He had promised to be by my side and comfort me when I finally stood at the spot where Nana left this earth. Where was he now? Georgina wondered. Where was her roommate now? Georgina ran her fingers through the grass. Did Nana's blood spill right here? If it did, it's all been washed away. Like every chance I had of living a normal happy life. She finished her cigarette, stubbed it out on the ground, then angrily threw the butt as far as she could.

"Well, Chip, it's time for your initiation into Georgina's club of cheating losers. I know you were just pretending to like me, like all the others. It always ends up the same way." She picked up the branding iron. Her hands were shaking.

46

Huck Darling and his bride, Isabelle, had been out with friends near his office on Wall Street when the blackout hit. They'd ended up having a great time. It turned into a big party at the restaurant where they were having dinner, and the owner gave them dessert for free. All the melting ice cream you could eat.

Luckily Huck had driven his car to work that morning. After dinner, he and Isabelle had dropped their oh-so-fabulous, socially connected friends at their pads around town, and were about to pull into the garage of their building when Huck's cell phone rang. It was his mother in New Jersey.

"Huck, our lights are back on."

"That's great, Mom. We're still in the dark. Isabelle and I are just about to pull into the garage and walk up twelve flights of stairs—"

Isabelle rolled her eyes. "It's going to be awful. And I'm wearing these heels . . ."

She's beautiful and rich but definitely high maintenance, Huck thought. For him, the whole package was more than worth it.

"If you're in the car, why don't you just drive out here? I'll turn the air conditioner on in your room. It'll be nice and cool when you get here."

"Mom, thanks for the offer, but it's already late and I have to get to work early tomorrow. It's a new job . . ."

"You'll have to go to work if there's a blackout?"

"Well, we won't know that until the morning, now will we?" he tried to joke.

Isabelle leaned over toward Huck's phone. "I think we should come to your house," she called out to her mother-in-law. "The thought of climbing up all those stairs to our hot, dark apartment filled with all those boxes . . ."

"You see, dear? Why don't you just drive on out? Make your bride happy."

Which is the worse of two evils? Huck wondered. Putting up with a cranky Isabelle in a hot apartment or facing a tough commute in the morning from New Jersey and risk being late for work?

Isabelle looked at him with a sour expression. "Well?"

47

Clay's cell phone rang as he and Lorraine were trudging down Sixth Avenue. He answered without checking to see who it was. Not good.

"Hey, dude, I know you were upset about your bicycle. But what did you do with Diane's tap shoes?"

"What are you talking about?"

"What do you mean what am I talking about? She took them off in the bathroom, and now they're gone."

"It's pretty dark in there. Take another look."

"We took a lot of looks. If you took them as some sort of joke to get even with her, okay. But bring them back now. She's very upset."

"I'll be home later."

"What is with you? She borrowed your bike because she really needed it. I know you're mad but you're overreacting."

"No, I'm not!" Clay shouted. "She had no right to use my bicycle without asking!"

"Clay, this is important. Her agent called. The producers of the show want to see her again first thing in the morning. She's been going crazy searching all over this apartment in the dark. She won't be able to sleep tonight if those shoes aren't back here."

Clay hung up and turned off his phone. "My room-mate thinks I took his girlfriend's shoes because I was mad about the flat tire. That's good. I'd grabbed them before I knew about the flat. Now at least I have an excuse."

"Whatever works." Lorraine sighed.

In the low Forties they headed west. Fire trucks came racing down the block past them, and screeched to a halt at the end of the block. Flames were shooting out of the windows of the fourth floor of a small apartment building. Tenants were standing on the sidewalk and a crowd was gathering.

A candle situated too close to a curtain had set it aflame. The apartment dwellers had done their best to get the fire under control but finally gave up and roused their fellow tenants.

Lorraine and Clay paused to watch the excitement. The flames lit up the night sky.

A woman near Lorraine gasped. Lorraine turned her head.

"Didn't I see you on *The Darkest Days*?" the older woman cried. She had her hair pulled back in a bun and was dressed in a long nightgown that was partially covered by a lightweight bathrobe. Her feet were stuffed into fluffy bedroom slippers.

Lorraine smiled. "Yes, I had a nice part on that last year. I was in several episodes."

"You don't have to tell me! That's my favorite soap opera of all time. They should bring your character back."

"Do you live in that building?" Clay asked with concern, trying to change the subject so they could make their exit. Now he was really desperate for the money to get a new apartment.

"Yes, it'll be fine," the woman answered dismissively. "They'll get it under control. I'm on the ground floor which doesn't seem to be affected." She turned back to Lorraine. "I'm going to write to the producers and tell them I saw you tonight, and they should bring you back—"

Lorraine cringed at the thought of letters to producers.

"—you were so convincing as a conniving you-know-what." The woman laughed, then pretended to whisper. "I won't tell them you were wearing ugly but comfortable shoes." She held up one foot. "I'm just like you, I love for my feet to feel good. I wear these all day at home. I can't bear to throw them out no matter how ratty they get."

Lorraine smiled through gritted teeth. "Thank you so much, but please don't write any letters to the producers. I'm about to start a film and will be very busy—"

"Which one?"

"Lorraine, we've really got to be going," Clay said.

"And who are you?" the woman demanded.

"I'm an actor, too."

"I've never seen you in anything."

"Oh, you will," Lorraine said quickly. "He's so talented. We really have to be going."

"Please just wait a minute. I want to get a picture with you. Someone around here must have a camera. My mother is not going to believe it . . ."

48

"Daddy, I feel terrible that we can't find him. No one has," Alexis said as she hung up her cell phone. She'd called Dodie, who said that there was no news and Chip's family was getting more and more upset.

"We'll keep looking, dear," Conrad promised as he steered the Rolls-Royce past the area on the West Side where the cruise ships docked. "It's so dark here at night . . ."

Alexis's cell phone rang. It was always ringing. This time it was her mother. "Alexis, where are you? I called your father's house and I was surprised you weren't there yet."

"Mom, you won't believe what happened," Alexis said, then gave her mother a rundown of the events of the last couple of hours. "Becky is with us. She saw the couple get in a cab in front of the comedy club."

"Alexis, be careful."

"We are. By the way, I think I saw Lorraine on the street near the Treetops Hotel."

Conrad looked at Alexis. "Did you have to bring that up to your mother?" he whispered.

"Daddy says I shouldn't have brought that up to you."

"What do I care? She's out on the street instead of hanging around the bar of the most expensive hotel in the city looking to meet producers? She must be up to something."

"Totally."

"Put your father on."

"Hello, dear," Conrad said wearily.

"I'm not going to give you a hard time," Penny assured him. "I just want to say it's great that you're helping search for that poor boy. Just be careful, please. And keep me updated. I'm not going to sleep until I know you're on your way home again."

Conrad felt his heart twinge. Could those words be prophetic?

49

A s Jack's car zoomed up the West Side Highway, the tension in the car was increasing.

"I wonder if Huck ever got married," Regan said. "We never asked Arthur if there was another name on the real estate documents."

"I wonder if he married the roommate," Kit scoffed.

"If he is married, then maybe he's more likely to be home," Jack reasoned.

They exited the highway at Seventy-second Street, made a quick left on West End Avenue and raced to the entrance of the Schwab House between Seventy-third and Seventy-fourth. The back of the building overlooked Riverside Drive, the West Side Highway, the Hudson River, and the cliffs of New Jersey.

Regan and Jack were the first ones to dash out of the car.

A doorman was sitting in the foyer, two lit candles on the table in front of him. He looked weary.

Jack quickly identified himself and showed the doorman his badge. "We need to speak to one of your residents, Huck Darling. It's very important. Do you know if he's home?"

The doorman snapped to attention. "You're in luck. He just got home, but his wife was trying to convince him to drive out to New Jersey. He wouldn't do it."

"What floor does he live on?" Jack demanded. "This is urgent."

"The twelfth. When you come out of the stairwell, his apartment is across the hall, first one to your left. But I don't think I can let a group of people . . ."

Jack grabbed Regan's hand. "Understood. My wife and I are going up. The others will wait down here."

They took the steps in the dimly lit stairwell two at a time. When they reached the twelfth floor, they ran out into the hallway, found Huck Darling's door, and rang the bell. Several times.

"Who's there?" a man called out.

"Jack Reilly from the NYPD. Please open up."

The door was opened a crack, but the chain was on. "Show me your badge."

Quickly Jack complied.

The man closed the door, unlatched the chain, and

opened it again. "What's going on?" he asked, alarm in his voice.

Regan immediately noticed his blond hair. An attractive woman was standing a few feet behind him. Several candles had been lit in the apartment. The lights of New Jersey were visible through the living room window.

"We're sorry to disturb you, but this is important," Jack explained. "Are you Huck Darling?"

"Yes."

"Did you know a Georgina Mathieson in college?"

"What?" the woman asked, stepping closer. "A Georgina who?"

"Yes, but not for long," Darling answered nervously, ignoring his wife.

"Did she tell you exactly where the accident that took her grandmother's life occurred?"

"I believe she did," he said slowly.

"You *believe* she did or she did?" Regan asked, already sure that she'd never like this guy. There was just something about him.

"She did tell me."

"Where was it?" Regan asked, her voice clipped.

He pointed out their living room window. "Right out there. On the West Side Highway just north of Seventy-second Street."

"Right there?" Regan asked, unable to hide the astonishment in her voice.

"Yes, I went to check it out once. That's what drew my attention to this building. I understand it was a terrible accident. I felt very sorry for Georgina, but I want you to know that Georgina was more than a little off—" he started to explain.

It was too late. Regan and Jack were gone. What a shameless jerk, Regan thought as she and Jack raced down the steps to the lobby.

50

Georgina was heating up the branding iron with her lighter. The black metal was getting hotter and hotter. I'd have made a great little girl scout, she thought, glancing at the words on the brand—I AM A SNAKE.

She started to get nervous and excited. She was breathing fast and her thoughts were racing. Being here at the spot where her grandmother died was making her even more agitated than she usually felt at this point.

Georgina positioned herself next to Chip's right arm. Wait a minute, she thought. He's a lefty. I noticed that tonight. It's much worse to have my brand on the arm you use most often. Just above the wrist, with the letters facing out for all the world to see.

She stood up and walked around the motionless body. "My first lefty," she whispered to him. "But certainly not my last."

51

"The accident happened on the West Side Highway right behind here!" Regan shouted to Kit, Melanie, and Billy, as she and Jack hurried out the front door of the Schwab House.

"Behind here?" Kit cried in disbelief. "And Georgina's ex lives in this building?"

"His apartment even has a view of the accident site," Regan said with disgust as she and Jack starting running to the corner, followed by Melanie.

Billy hesitated. "Kit, I don't want to leave you alone . . ."

"I'll be okay!" Kit insisted. "Go ahead! I'll catch up with you."

Billy turned and took off, joining the sprint down Seventy-third Street to Riverside Park. The park was a narrow, scenic, four-mile strip of land between the Hudson River and Riverside Drive. It began at Seventy-second Street, where the West Side Highway became the Henry Hudson Parkway, and stretched four miles.

"Wait a second," Jack instructed after they all reached the park's entrance at Seventy-second Street, where a statue of Eleanor Roosevelt greeted them. "It's so dark here it's impossible to see a foot in front of you without a flashlight. Let's spread out a little and cover this area just north of Seventy-second Street without losing sight of each other's lights. If

Georgina's in the park, let's hope she didn't wander too far from the scene of the accident, which I gather happened right up there." He pointed to the highway where cars were speeding past the spot that had changed Georgina's life.

Silently, the four of them fanned out.

She's got to be very close to here, Regan thought as she hurried down a grassy knoll toward the highway underpass. If Georgina's grandmother was thrown from a car above, depending on which direction she was traveling, she either landed right around here, or on the other side of the underpass closer to the river. Georgina may have wanted to take Chip down by the waterfront where it's even more isolated. And if she left him there and he woke up disoriented, he could end up falling in and drowning. I have to look over there now, Regan thought with a sudden urgency. She turned, about to call out to Jack. But a sound, almost imperceptible, made her stop in her tracks.

Several feet from Regan, behind a cluster of bushes, Georgina was on the ground facing the stone wall that extended up to the side of the highway. She had just flicked off her lighter. Staring at its flame as she heated up the brand and her total absorption in the task had put her into a trancelike state. With her right hand she was holding on tight to the handle of the scalding hot brand. Chip's left arm was perfectly still on the ground. Narrowing her eyes, Georgina positioned the brand and aimed it at his skin.

"Stop!" a woman's voice screamed as a light from

behind suddenly illuminated the sickening sight.

Startled, a wild-eyed Georgina turned her head toward the source of the light, then quickly turned her attention back to Chip. But it was too late. Arms reached around her torso, pulled her up, and yanked her back away from Chip's body.

Thank God, Regan thought, as they both fell backward to the ground, Georgina's body landing on top of hers. Georgina, holding on to the branding iron more tightly than ever, started screaming as she twisted her body and flailed her arms, desperately trying to break free of Regan's grasp.

"Regan!" Jack yelled as he raced toward them.

"Watch out! The brand!"

In an instant, Jack, Melanie, and Billy were just feet away.

"Train your flashlights on them!" Jack ordered.

"Ahhhh," Regan yelled as a corner of the brand grazed her left arm. With all her might, her arms around Georgina's waist, Regan rolled their bodies to the right.

Georgina extended her right arm outward as they rolled, keeping the brand a safe distance from herself. With lightning speed, Jack lunged forward and forcefully brought his foot down on Georgina's right forearm, pinning it to the ground. He reached out and grabbed her left wrist, holding it tight.

"Let go of the brand!" he commanded.

"You're hurting me!" she wailed, her fingers grasping the brand.

"I said let go."

Jack's foot pressed down harder on her arm. She cried out in pain and released her grip. Jack reached down, picked the brand up, and quickly handed it over to Billy. "Regan, are you okay?" he asked as he pulled Georgina to her feet and snapped a pair of handcuffs around her wrists. "Did you get burned?"

"Just barely," Regan answered as she scrambled over to Chip's body, tried to shake him awake, then grabbed his wrist. "His pulse is low," she cried. "He won't wake up. Call an ambulance."

"I already did," Kit shouted as she crutched down the hill. "They're on their way. I think it's coming now."

As the sound of the approaching ambulance grew louder, Jack growled to Georgina, "You'd better pray that this guy makes it. What did you slip him?"

"I didn't give him anything!" she protested. "We had a couple of drinks, that's all."

Regan held Chip's hand and tapped his face. "Come on, Chip. There are a lot of people who love you and are so worried. Your parents and your sister and your friend Phil . . . there were search parties of people you don't even know out looking for you tonight . . . they can't wait to see you and talk to you . . ."

The ambulance screeched to a halt on Riverside Drive, followed by several patrol cars. Paramedics hurried into the park with a stretcher. As Regan explained what happened, they quickly placed an oxygen mask on Chip's face, took his vital signs, and gave him a shot of flumazenil. "We'll get him to the hospital."

"Is he going to be all right?" Regan asked anxiously. Jack was standing next to her, his arm draped protectively around her shoulder. Kit and Billy were standing a few feet away.

One of the emergency medical workers nodded. "I think so. His vital signs are okay. If she did slip him chloral hydrate and he was drinking alcohol, he'll be out of it for a while. But he's young and looks strong."

Regan sighed with relief. "I'll contact his family. We'll meet you at the hospital."

"Yes, ma'am. St. Luke's," he said as the paramedics started wheeling the stretcher out of the park.

Jack pulled Regan close. "Are you sure you're okay? You yelped in pain. Let me see where she got you." He shone his flashlight on her left arm. An angry red mark stood in stark contrast to Regan's pale skin. "Regan! Look at that!"

"Oh, Regan!" Kit echoed.

Regan shrugged. "I'm just so grateful she didn't drop that brand on Chip or throw it at his face when I grabbed her. Can you imagine if . . ."

Melanie came running toward them. She had gotten cold water and an icepack from the ambulance. "Here, Regan, this is for your arm. The paramedics couldn't believe you didn't tell them you were burned."

"I didn't want them to waste time on me. Honestly, it's just now that I'm starting to feel it. It doesn't hurt much," Regan insisted, as Jack took the water and poured it over her arm. "That does feel good, though. I've gotten burns much worse than this when I've tried to cook dinner," she joked. "Remember, Kit?"

Kit smiled. "Yes, I do."

"Now, if she had branded me with I AM A SNAKE, then I'd be upset."

Jack shook his head as he tenderly held the icepack against her arm.

Regan smiled. "Listen, everybody. I'm really okay. We've got to get to the hospital. Let's go." She reached into her pocket for her cell phone as they started to move. "And before another minute passes, I've got to make some very important phone calls."

Georgina was ahead of them, being led out of the park in handcuffs. A small group was gathered on the sidewalk, watching the events unfold. Georgina barely glanced at them, but her brain registered a flicker of familiarity, and she looked again. The color drained from her face. It was as if she'd seen a ghost.

In a way, she had.

Huck Darling was standing just a few feet away.

"I'm sorry, Georgina," he said as he approached her. "I didn't mean to hurt you . . ."

Georgina glared at him, and with a perfect aim, spit in his face. As the onlookers gasped, she got in the back of the patrol car.

52

"Well, we're almost there, finally!" Clay said testily. "Did you have to spend so much time talking to that woman about your fan club?"

"If she wants to start one, I couldn't be rude."

"I hate to tell you, but if you don't get those letters back, there won't be a need for a fan club."

"Call the Reillys again and make sure they aren't home."

Clay did as he was told. "No answer. Maybe they're out of town. That would be a treat."

As they approached Tribeca, the streetlights flickered on. "Oh, no!" Lorraine cried. "It would have been better for us if the power were still off and the Reillys' building was dark!"

Clay shook his head. "I told you not to waste time. It's just a couple more blocks. Let's hope the key still works. If it does, we'll get in and out and be on our way. Do you think you can jog?"

"Of course I can," she insisted, even though the sides of the borrowed shoes were chafing her skin. Mind over matter, she thought as they ran down the narrow street. We're almost there.

53

Sue and Chris Jones were driving in agonized silence. It was too painful for either of them to talk. They were both praying for the safe return of their son. As they were traveling on the Massachusetts Turnpike, the ring of their cell phone through the car speakers made them both flinch. Regan Reilly's number appeared on the dashboard screen. Sue steepled her hands and closed her eyes as Chris answered.

"Regan?"

"Yes. We found Chip! He's unconscious but the paramedics think he's going to be fine."

A cry of relief emanated from Sue's mouth. Her head fell to her knees. Chris's eyes blinked back tears. "Oh, Regan," Sue said as she slowly sat back up. "Thank you. Thank you. Did she—"

"No, she didn't brand him. It was a little close for comfort, but we got there in time."

"Thank you, God," Sue whispered.

"Where is Chip now?" Chris asked.

"An ambulance is taking him to St. Luke's Hospital on the west side of Manhattan. It's on Amsterdam Avenue, two blocks west of Columbus Circle."

"We're going to get there as soon as we can," Chris said. "It'll be a few more hours, which will seem like forever to us. But nothing can be as bad as the last few."

"Godspeed."

54

Arthur was fit to be tied. Zora had stopped in the bathroom on the way out of One Police Plaza and had taken her sweet time.

"All this excitement. My tummy's a little off," she explained when she finally climbed in the back of Wally's car.

Spare me any details, Arthur had thought. Regan and Jack had taken off several minutes earlier, and Arthur had the feeling that every minute counted.

When Wally's car finally approached the exit off the West Side Highway at Seventy-second Street, the flashing lights of several patrol cars stopped at Riverside Park came into view.

"There they are!" Arthur cried, pointing to Regan and Jack. He punched the seat. "We missed everything!"

Wally stopped the car. "Oh there's Rod," he said. "He made it."

"Who cares?" Arthur mumbled as he jumped out and hurried over to Regan, who was getting off her cell phone.

"Arthur!" she said, greeting him with a hug. "Thank God you found Huck's address. Georgina was right here in Riverside Park with Chip. We arrived just in time. One more minute and she would have scarred him for life. She must have drugged him—he was out cold—but he's going to be okay."

Inwardly Arthur fumed. That idiot Zora, he thought. "I'm glad I could be of help," he muttered.

"You can't imagine how Chip's parents feel. They are beside themselves with relief. And his friend Phil is racing over to the hospital right now. He wants to have a celebration party tomorrow night at Lonnie's, the bar on the Upper East Side where the search parties were formed. You have to come. They are all going to want to meet you and thank you for what you made possible."

Conrad's Rolls-Royce pulled up.

Jack slapped Arthur on the back. "Arthur, I think I should offer you a job. You can do no wrong, buddy."

"Yes, I can."

"Oh, Arthur, don't be so modest," Regan teased.

"I have a confession to make."

"No!" Wally moaned. "Please don't!"

Uh-oh, Rod thought. I'm afraid I know what's coming.

"I can't live with myself if I don't come right out with it."

"With what?" Regan asked.

"I was the one in your apartment tonight."

Regan blinked. "You?"

"It's true. I was the one who locked you out on the roof. Wally discovered a hidden safe in your new apartment. We just wanted to see if there was anything in it that you wouldn't have missed anyway because you didn't know about it. That's *all* I was doing there. Wally said it was the contractor's ultimate fantasy to find hidden treasures at a renovation site. Well, it's been a nightmare for me!"

"What?" Conrad bellowed. "A hidden safe? Where?"

"In the front closet."

"Daddy!" Alexis squealed. "I bet you Lorraine had it installed. And I bet that's where she was headed when we saw her on the street!"

"Why would she be going there now?" Regan asked.

"It was just tonight that I broke the news to her that I sold the loft. She's been in England for three months."

"And we never changed the keys," Jack blurted.

They all jumped in their cars and raced down to Tribeca.

55

Lorraine and Clay had entered the building with her key, which thankfully still worked. They snuck up the stairs to the apartment. When her second key opened the door to the apartment, her knees went weak.

"Here we go," she whispered as they stepped inside.

Carefully and quietly, they crossed the room to the closet. As Clay held the flashlight, Lorraine squatted down, removed the false wall, and entered the code to the safe—0101, for her January first birthday. The safe beeped, and she turned the key.

As she pulled open the door, Clay was trying to

decide which area of town he'd look in for a new apartment.

For the second time in an hour, Regan and Jack were racing up a stairwell. At the door to their new apartment Jack turned the key and flicked on the lights.

A gasp was heard from the closet, and the door was quickly yanked shut.

Jack rolled his eyes and hurried over. He pulled on the door. "Come out with your hands up!" he ordered.

The door slowly opened. Lorraine Lily and her cohort were standing there in shock.

"She's here!" Alexis cried gleefully as she pulled out her cell phone and began to record the proceedings. "Becky, is this awesome or what? My mother is going to love this! Especially the sight of those awful shoes!"

"Those shoes are shocking," Becky agreed.

"Out!" Jack ordered.

"The stuff in the safe is mine!" Lorraine screamed. "I came back to get what belongs to me!"

"What's going on?" Clay protested. "Lorraine, you mean you don't live here any more?" He turned to the others. "We rehearsed here several times. We were scene partners—"

"You're a lousy actor, Clay," Lorraine screeched. "You were in on this with me and you know it."

Conrad shook his head, delighted at the scene. "Oh, Lorraine, I'm so surprised at you. Now what's in that safe anyway? Some of the money you withdrew from my accounts?"

"All I want are my letters," Lorraine protested.

"What?" Clay gasped.

"They must be *some* letters," Conrad said. "I can't wait to read them."

"No!"

"I'll make a deal with you. You can have your letters back if you agree you don't want a cent of alimony, or any part of the house. We'll keep the letters in a safe-deposit box in case you change your mind and take me to court. Of course, the Reillys have to decide if they want to press charges . . ."

Wally and Arthur and Rod were standing by the door with Kit and Billy and Melanie and Zora and Leon.

"Well, well. If they catch the stinker who broke into our gallery, it would be a perfect end to the evening," Zora said. "Wouldn't it, dear?"

"The perfect ending," Leon agreed, nodding his head up and down.

Rod turned to Wally. "Thanks for ruining my business. You and your friend here."

"He saved me from ruin!" Conrad said gleefully. "Don't worry, Rod. This won't ruin your business. I'll make sure you get plenty of work. And I'll be glad to pay for any lawyers. If Arthur hadn't confessed, we wouldn't have caught Lorraine up to her tricks."

"And if it weren't for Arthur, we never would have gotten our beautiful statues back," Zora said.

The room was silent for a moment.

"Arthur, was it your stun gun?" Regan asked.

"Yes. But I would never ever have used it on you,

Regan. Never would I have zapped you! And I bought it in a state where they're legal."

56

It was daybreak when Chip's parents came racing into the hospital. "Our son, Chip Jones. Where is he?"

The attendant smiled. "He's been waiting for you. Follow me."

Sue and Chris clasped each other's hands and were led through the emergency room. The attendant finally stopped and pulled away a curtain. Phil was sound asleep in the chair next to Chip's bed.

Chip smiled weakly and pointed at his friend. "Can you believe the nerve of this guy?"

Tears in their eyes, they both laughed and reached down for what they knew would be the best hug of their lives.

July 15th, 9 p.m.

57

The next night there was quite a celebration at Lonnie's. Power had been restored to New York City, and Chip was back in the company of his family, friends, and a group of new friends whom he would never forget. His sister had flown in from California on the first flight possible.

"I would have walked here," she told Regan. "Thanks so much."

"Natalie, it wasn't just me. As you can see there were a lot of people who were out looking for your brother," Regan said as she glanced around the bar.

Conrad was next to his ex-wife, Penny, his arm around the back of her chair. Alexis was beaming. "I'm going to invite everyone here to my birthday party. Dad, don't forget. The party's a week from Saturday."

"Of course I won't forget! Maybe I'd better come home with you and your mother tonight and help with all the plans," he suggested, squeezing his ex-wife's shoulder.

Penny sipped her drink. "I have girlfriends who would never speak to me again if I took you back."

"Who cares what they think?" Conrad leaned over and kissed her cheek.

She raised her eyebrows and laughed.

Never say never, Conrad thought hopefully.

Kit and Billy were on stools at the bar, finally getting a chance to know each other. Wouldn't that be nice? Regan thought. Phil had his arm around Dodie. Melanie was telling everyone she wanted to move to New York. Becky was toasting Chip's foray into comedy. Larry had made room for him in the first class. Chip and his parents happily clinked glasses.

Nora and Luke had arrived from Los Angeles that afternoon. "Regan, I can't believe we missed everything," Nora said. "But I'm glad we're here for the celebration."

Rod and Wally and Arthur were stuck at a corner table with Zora and Leon. Zora was chewing their ears off. "And, Arthur, I think if anyone is going to catch that bandit who stole our sculptures, it will be you. I just know it. I'm telling you, if you just put your mind to it . . ."

Jack smiled and looked at Regan. "Honey, I can't believe we're letting them get away with breaking into our apartment."

"But, Jack," Regan said with a glint in her eye. "We'll be the first people in the history of renovations who have their apartment finished on time." She glanced over at Wally and Rod, who both looked a little glum. "Something tells me it might even be ready early . . ."

Laughing, Jack leaned down and kissed her. "Regan, I don't care where I live or under what conditions . . . as long as I'm with you."

Center Point Publishing
600 Brooks Road ● PO Box 1
Thorndike ME 04986-0001 USA

(207) 568-3717

US & Canada:
1 800 929-9108
www.centerpointlargeprint.com